ENCOUNTER WITH TERROR

"Hello, Alfie," the figure said in a strange and hollow voice.

Alfie quivered at the sound of his own name. How did the shadow know him so well?

The face of the man came into the light and Alfie whimpered. He had never seen the face before. At least he couldn't remember. But the stranger had called him by name.

"I don't know you," he whined. "How'd you know my name?"

"Been a long time, Alfie. Don't you remember?"

Alfie retreated a step and looked about for an escape route. The lantern slipped from his hand, and he stumbled back along the wooden walk. "Get away from me," he screamed. "Don't touch me. I didn't do nothin'."

The man from the car picked up the lantern, and it streaked his dark suit and stern face with flared wedges of light.

Alfie floundered. He bumped against the cracked candy-cane pole of the old barber shop and fled past the shattered window of the long-vacant pool hall. When his foot twisted in the rotted planking, he fell to his knees before the ghostly figure that trailed him by only a dozen paces.

He was screaming. He knew that, but the street was whirling around him. He could even hear another man's voice; but he couldn't understand why the light kept coming closer, ever closer. . . .

WRITE FOR OUR FREE CATALOG

If there is a Pinnacle Book you want—and you cannot find it locally—it is available from us simply by sending the title and price plus 50¢ per order and 10¢ per copy to cover mailing and handling costs to:

> Pinnacle Books, Inc.
> Reader Service Department
> 2029 Century Park East
> Los Angeles, California 90067

Please allow 4 weeks for delivery. New York State and California residents add applicable sales tax.

_____Check here if you want to receive our catalog regularly.

BRANNON!
Daniel T. Streib

PINNACLE BOOKS   LOS ANGELES

This is a work of fiction. All the characters and events portrayed in this book are fictional, and any resemblance to real people or incidents is purely coincidental.

BRANNON!

Copyright © 1973 by Daniel T. Streib

All rights reserved, including the right to reproduce this book or portions there of in any form.

An original Pinnacle Books edition, published for the first time anywhere.

First printing, January 1973
Second printing, August 1980

ISBN: 0-523-40512-X

Cover illustration by Len Goldberg

Printed in the United States of America

PINNACLE BOOKS, INC.
2029 Century Park East
Los Angeles, California 90067

To my wife,
who discovered Timberland for me.

BRANNON!

1952

CHAPTER 1

"Fuck!" Sid Webster grunted to himself as he squeezed his fat ass from between the arms of the battered swivel chair. Pain slithered up his back from the fused vertebrae near his tail bone, as his sixty-year-old muscles resisted their first exercise within hours.

The ache at the back of his head and the faint quivering of his forked hands impelled him to shuffle across the warped floor of the barren station. His head always ached and his hands shook more noticeably whenever he had gone too long without drink.

And today had been a particularly long period of abstinence. He had coaxed the last of the rye from the coke bottle in his room before noon. But the shaking hadn't grown pronounced until the clock above the single passenger bench had clicked past eight-thirty.

"They should be back by now," he told himself. "Bastards. They got no consideration."

The clock clacked again, a small hammer tapping

sharply at his skull. Time dragged when you needed a drink. He had tried everything, even twisting the gooseneck lamp on the dispatcher's desk until it focused on the calendar beneath the clock.

January. It was always January in Timberland's frame depot. Years before, someone had ruled that the blonde above the chain-saw company's imprint was bare enough to arouse a man's imagination without arousing the righteous ire of the few women who occasionally entered the station. But tonight even Miss January had failed to take his mind off the drink. For revenge he aimed his rear at her big boobs and farted.

At the window he cupped his hands around his eyes and pressed his strawberry-shaped nose against the glass. When he thought he saw a spot of light far down the track, he grunted impatiently and shuffled outside onto the ramp.

The night air was balmy for June. At this altitude the warmth of the day escaped with the sun, but tonight the absence of a breeze and the surrounding wall of pines had combined to create a kettle that left the town simmering.

Holding his meaty arms out like wings to let air to sweaty, matted hair beneath his shoulders, he leaned out over the tracks. In the distance, across the glimmering millpond, he could hear the buzz of the saws slicing through timber; behind him he could hear rousing hymns from the auditorium. But it was the saucy toot of a train whistle far down the tracks that caused a dribble of urine to escape into his undershorts.

God, he needed a drink.

The whistle tooted again and Sid Webster fretted.

He didn't want anyone to know, he mumbled to himself. That fool Alfie. No sense at all.

Brazenly, with its single eye glaring up the curving channel through the cone-shaped trees, the small yard engine chugged into the station, braked, and hissed out its last breath for the night.

From the open cab came the boisterous laughter of men full of drink.

Sid Webster fretted again, fearing that his errand boys had consumed what he had sent them to get. But as the first figure dropped to the ramp, Webster could see the brown paper sack held gingerly under an elbow, and he knew he would have to endure the pain in his head for only a few minutes more.

Deliberately Webster pinched the end of his nose with his thumb and forefinger and blew snot at his feet. Until he had recognized the first figure to descend from the cab, he had not felt the moisture in his nostrils. The gesture was strictly for Stephen Grossett, the tall, slender boy of twenty who approached through the exhaling steam of the engine.

Grossett, though he never openly showed it, cringed at the crudities of the warped man who tended the town's depot. In college, Grossett escaped the rawness of the lumberman and their uneducated women who inhabited the company-owned structures of the town, but it was summer and he had no choice but to come home.

The fragile hands of the boy held out the wrapped bottle of rye. Webster took it without thanks.

Behind Grossett came Scott Cameron, unshaven, a little drunk, his dungarees worn thin at the knees and his best flannel shirt faded from a hundred washings. His hair, still crew-cut by his mother, and the glint of naiveté in his eyes suggested his youth, although his plump face was already weathering from the five years he had spent in the woods since dropping out of school.

In his hands, cuddled like a nursing baby, he clutched a second bottle, its broad base wrapped protectively in the huge cups of a lady's bra.

Behind him the engine whistle tooted again, its voice choking but still loud with the exhausting steam.

Irritably Scott Cameron shouted back at the open cab. "Cram it, Alfie. You'll wake the whole motherfuckin' town."

"It's my engine, ain't it?" Alfie shouted from the cab. "Ma bought it for me, didn't she?"

"Screw your ma," Cameron snorted, as he started up the ramp.

At the engine, Alfie coaxed one more toot from the whistle, then swung down out of the cab.

"Hey, you guys, wait for me," he pleaded.

Unneeded now that his engine had transported the others to Chestertown and back, he had to jog to catch up, his Coleman lantern bobbing at his side.

His body, six feet of firm muscle and strong bones, wobbled as he ran and his frizzled head seemed to flop uncontrollably at the end of a disproportionately long and bony neck.

Reaching the others, he clutched at Cameron's arm for reassurance. "She did, didn't she? She bought the engine just for me. Right?"

Cameron snorted again. "Yeah. Like she built the movie theater just for you, you and your damned Snow White and Gulliver's Travels and all that kid crap."

Alfie whined weakly, then was still as Sid Webster scowled at him without approval.

"You get two?" he asked of Cameron.

Cameron unsheathed the second bottle and held the bra aloft by its strap. "Got this too," he said proudly.

"He got it off a mannikin," Steve Grossett added, his high-pitched voice as belittling as possible. "Broke a window to get it."

Undaunted, Cameron slung the big cups down below his waist. "Look, maybe I could use it as a jock strap. Just about right for me."

"I want it, I want it," Alfie cried, his big stiff fingers snatching at the bra until he could clutch it to his nose. "Smells like a woman," he said.

Moving away with the others, Grossett called over his shoulder, "How would you know, Alfie? You ever been with a woman?"

"Because I know, that's why. I ain't so dumb. My folks own this town. Gettin' borned to people like that, that ain't so dumb."

Ahead of Alfie the procession stumbled across the tracks, passed the town hall with its steepled bell tower, and moved up the main street. Several dozen cars, all caked with the gray mud of California, lined the oiled road, and domed lights overhead created a mosaic of glare and sharp-lined shadows. But the plank walks were empty of people.

At the barber shop the lighted candy cane continued its relentless upward twist, but inside, the swivel chair waited with the cover cloth draped across an arm. In the window of the grocery, the neon bread sign sizzled and blinked; at the Mobil station, the flying red horse still pranced in the beam of a spotlight. Other shops, all housed in gray frame buildings in the style of Monopoly-set hotels, displayed their wares to an empty street through fly-specked windows.

Down the street, the movie theater—a four-story, peaked-roof building of local timber—was dark, its marquee stripped of plastic letters. From the auditorium, though, came the sounds of a slightly off-tuned piano. A courtly building with huge oaken doors (the only imported wood in town), the auditorium sparkled with lights from its narrow ventilating windows high on the upper stories. Outside, spot-lighted with two yellowish beams, a chalk board proclaimed the event in broad white strokes—Recital Tonight.

Back at the grocery store, the four men from the depot cautiously arranged themselves on the porch, the older man named Webster in the enameled rocking chair and the others around him at respectable distances.

Comfortable again, Webster uncorked the rye bottle and brought it to his lips. The others watched intently.

Only when the older man had paused for breath, did Steve Grossett break the reverent silence. "Mr. Ward sees that bottle, we're all dead," he mused.

Scott Cameron blew air through his nose in a blast of bravado. "He don't own the world."

"Yes, he does," Alfie proclaimed defensively. "Pa owns everything . . . the stores, the houses, the church, the mill."

"Timberland ain't the world," Cameron insisted.

Webster wiped imaginary dirt from the bottle mouth with the sleeve of his shirt. "Might as well be," he said.

Alfie Ward had more to say, but a burst of applause from the auditorium took all their attention from him, and as one they saw the shaft of light from an open door at the rear of the building.

Quickly Webster stashed the bottle in the shadow of his arms as a figure of a girl left the auditorium, passed the bachelor's bunkhouse and cut across a vacant lot opposite the store.

"Hey, sis," Alfie cried out. "Where you going?"

Squeamishly, the others silenced him and didn't relax until the figure in the white frock disappeared into the darkness.

"Damned fool," Webster barked, then turned accusingly on Cameron. "You give him any that booze?"

Cameron looked hurt. "Naw! He's goofy enough."

Webster grunted and then coughed as another swig burned his throat. "Get some beer," he ordered.

When no one moved, Cameron turned on Grossett. "You, college boy. Get us some beer."

"Yeah, college boy," Alfie echoed. "Get us some beer."

Steve Grossett hesitated and then welcomed the escape. The effects of the drinks they'd had in Chestertown were wearing off rapidly; once more he could smell the dried sweat in the other men's clothes.

With Grossett disappearing into the store, Cameron and Webster concentrated on the bottle until they heard the grating of gears from the hill just outside of town.

"Bus is coming," Alfie observed, as he spotted the powerful lights cutting through the trees.

Sid Webster leaned forward in his chair. "It's turnin' in off'n the highway. Somebody must've flagged it."

"Naw," Cameron said, but even as he spoke the bus turned onto the main street, rumbled down toward them, and belched to a stop in front of the store.

The air brakes hissed and the door popped open. An army duffel bag flew out. A second later the silhouetted figure of a soldier came stumbling out. Behind him the uniformed driver cursed him, "Hoof it, you goddamned punk. Sixty miles through the fragrant pines."

Stooped to recover the shirts and shaving gear that spilled from his bag, the soldier raised his hand in a one-fingered salute.

Bristling with curiosity, Scott Cameron stepped to the bus and questioned the driver. "What's with him?"

"He had a broad," the driver mumbled, "half-naked, spread out on the back seat."

"Pig?" Cameron asked hopefully.

"Naw, damn him. She's a doll."

The driver slammed the door and moved back to his seat. On the porch as the bus pulled away, Alfie Ward squinted toward the unfamiliar figure. "Who's that, Mr. Webster?" he asked.

"Don't know, Alfie," Webster told him.

"Thought you knowed everybody."

Rocking forward on his chair, Webster cocked his head. The light from the store window glared behind him, yet somehow the newcomer's face remained shadowed. He was young, Webster could tell that, and lean, but he could see little more, only the trim lines of a uniform. "Hey, looka here," the older man crowed. "A soldier boy. Fresh from Korea maybe. Got your arse goosed off the bus, didn't you, boy?"

"He must have," Steve Grossett said from the doorway. "Why else would anybody get off in Timberland?"

Coming outside, Steve handed one opened beer to Webster and drank from the other.

As Steve lowered the bottle from his mouth, the soldier set his bag aside and brazenly took the beer for himself. "Hey," Grossett protested. He stretched out his arm to snatch back the bottle, but he had to jerk his hand aside as the soldier spit out the warm beer.

"Beer leaves me cooler than that," the soldier grumbled.

Delighted, Alfie Ward screamed approval and danced around the pillar to the porch roof until Cameron slapped him heartily between the shoulder blades.

"Cut that out," Alfie grumbled, before retreating down the wooden porch into the shadows.

He stayed there sulking as Webster poured a slug of the rye into his own beer bottle and passed that across to the soldier. "How come you got dumped, soldier. Ain't the bus line behind our fightin' men no more?"

"Dumb broad," the soldier said between swallows.

"Ran my hand up her skirt and she got to giggling."

Cameron gaped incredulously. "You done that?"

"And they left you in Ward's town?" Steve Grossett smirked. "Better start walking, soldier. There's twelve miles of Adam Ward timber between here and anywhere else."

"Who's Ward?"

Alfie bounded up the porch again, his limp arms flapping at his side. "The whole town, that's all."

"The lumber mill," Webster began, "the rail spur, the town hall . . . it's all his."

"The whiskey too?" the soldier asked coolly.

Webster and Cameron winced, glancing nervously toward the halfwit behind them.

"That ain't whiskey," Alfie said authoritatively. "It's cleanin' fluid for your insides, ain't it, Mr. Webster?"

Steve Grossett smiled weakly. "Mr. Ward doesn't allow whiskey in Timberland."

"He don't like fast-fingered studs much neither," Cameron contributed.

From the chair came the light laughter of Sid Webster. "He's so straightlaced, he figures a virgin birth is the only proper kind."

"And you done that on the bus."

"Right up her skirt?"

"You wishin' you done that, Grossett?" Alfie taunted.

Scott Cameron spit towards the street, a gesture of contempt he had seen once in a movie. "Not Steve Grossett. Girls scare 'im. Don't know how he's gonna be a doctor and do all them nice things to women."

"Shut up, Cameron."

"You gonna make me?"

The two moved together threateningly, but the soldier ignored them. "There's a hotel, I suppose. Somewhere I can spend the night."

Cameron shook his head. "Ain't no hotel. No U.S.O. neither."

"Pa gives everybody an apartment," Alfie said defensively. "He don't even charge 'em much rent."

Steve Grossett chuckled cynically. "Sure. Two rooms of unpainted lumber and only a quick sprint to the outhouse."

"How about women?" the soldier asked. "Got anything special in that line?"

"Naw."

"Nothing."

"You kiddin'?" Alfie pouted and ran his hand down across his fly. "We ain't got no women worth mentionin'."

"The hell we ain't," Sid Webster drooled.

The others turned sharply, staring at him as though they suspected him of some diabolical intrigue.

"Who?" Cameron demanded.

"Yeah, who?"

"Catherine," Webster answered firmly.

"Who?"

Sid Webster drank again before he repeated himself. This time he spoke with deliberate clarity. "The Ward girl."

"My sister?" Alfie shrieked.

"You kidding?"

"She's cute, ain't she?"

Scott Cameron considered the question and answered slowly for everybody. "Yeah, she's cute."

"Got a good shape, right?"

"Sure, she's smart too, but . . ."

"Not one of you wouldn't like to get to her, is there?"

"Yeah, but . . ."

"But what?"

"She's a Ward," Steve Grossett answered sharply. Alfie agreed. "Right. Shes a Ward."

"She married?" the soldier asked.

Sid Webster rocked back in his chair. "Not married. Not engaged. Not nothin'."

"One of you sampling her regular?"

"Nobody diddles that," Scott Cameron snapped. "Not likely neither."

"Why not?" the soldier asked and a veiled note of self-confidence in his voice incensed the men around him.

"You think you're something special?" Cameron challenged. "Just cause you run your hand up some whore's skirt."

"You some kinda expert in this line, soldier boy?"

"Maybe."

"Care to prove that?"

The soldier shrugged and pushed his duffel bag forward to fill the gap between them. "Okay. A duffel bag full of souvenirs against a ride out of here."

"Alfie'll give you a life," Cameron sneered. "In his locomotive . . . tootin' all the way."

"Sure," Alfie squealed. "I'll let you toot her if you want."

Sid Webster rocked back in the chair and crossed his legs. Better than Miss January down at the station, he thought. "You got a deal, soldier. Screw the Ward girl and we'll ride you outa town in style."

"You can't bet on a thing like that," Steve Grossett roared. "Catherine's no poker chip."

"Just cause you can't get to her . . ." Cameron sneered.

"That's got nothing to do with it."

"Sure."

"You gotta make out tonight," Webster told the soldier. "By midnight or your lose."

"Just point me at her," the soldier said, and around him the men shuffled their feet.

Then Alfie giggled. He rubbed his fly and giggled. "But what'll I do then?"

"Take the soldier over there," Webster ordered. "Show him where she lives, Scott. Show him good."

"You do nothing. Watch, but stay outa sight."

"J-e-s-u-s!" Alfie gasped. "We get to watch?"

"You mind a big audience?" Webster asked the soldier.

"Not as long as they're quiet."

"All right. All of you. Only give him a fair shake."

Alfie danced off the porch and ran into the street. Waving his arms and flopping his head, he cried at the sky. "Sis is gonna get it. Sis is gonna get it. Sis is gonna get it good."

"She's a doll," Cameron said as he hooked his hand in the soldier's elbow and pulled him from the store. "A livin' doll. Got a shape won't quit."

On the porch, Steve Grossett hesitated, the half empty beer bottle hanging at his side. "You coming?" he asked the older man in the chair.

Webster shook his head and took another drink.

"Ward'll find out," Grossett's high-pitched voice whined. "Alfie'll tell."

Webster stared out into the street. He didn't seem to hear.

"If you go," he said, "keep Alfie quiet. He'll be squealin' louder'n the matin' call of a bull moose."

"Damn!" Grossett said, but he stepped off the porch and headed up the street.

Ahead of him the soldier walked with a stiff self-assurance. On his right walked Cameron, his own voice growing higher-pitched with excitement. "You'll never do it," he insisted. "She's no slut."

"I get to sit the closest," Alfie pleaded. "She's my sister.'

CHAPTER 2

Across the log-choked pond, the mill hummed, buzzed and clanked in the even stillness of the night. Closer by a frog croaked, an owl hooted, and in the black water between the floating chips of bark, a bluegill surfaced, mouthed a cisco fly and dove for the shallow bottom.

Somewhere a dog barked.

At the privet hedge around the sprawling house of Adam Ward, the four men paused.

"There she is," Alfie whisperd.

His big hand flapped like a flag and pointed toward a wisp of white, standing in the shadows of the pyracantha.

"She won't do it," Steve Grossett said. His voice was loud, almost loud enough to be heard at the house.

The others pulled him down. They huddled together behind the bushes while the soldier left them and ambled up the winding walk toward the girl. He seemed to be in no hurry.

"Evening," the soldier said.

"Is that you, Alfie?" they heard her ask.

"You frightened me." Her voice was muffled, but they filled in the words for themselves. "I don't know you. But I know everybody in Timberland."

Then the words grew fainter yet and the men at the hedge squirmed for better positions.

"What's happening now?" Grossett asked from his position farthest back toward the street. "I can't see a thing."

"They're talking."

"I didn't think she talked to anybody any more."

Alfie giggled. "Not since she started wearin' a brassiere, she ain't."

"Well, she's talkin' to him all right."

"Just being polite," Grossett said.

"Real polite. Look at her now."

Steve Grossett slithered across the moist grass near the hedge until he could see.

Even at a distance he could tell. She was standing closer to him now, not backing away at all.

"You're a strange boy," she was saying, "coming up to somebody's house like this. Usually I don't talk to strangers."

Brazenly Scott Cameron rose to his knees and crawled around the edge of the bushes. The others came with him, pressing their elbows into his sides as if out of fear. "Look," he whispered. "She's kinda squirmin' already. Wanting to get close."

Alfie squirmed uncomfortably, tugging at the front of his pants. He had an erection, which was tangled painfully in the flap of his undershorts, but he had no intention of looking away from the couple at the house.

"You really know women, don't you, Cameron?" he said in awe. "I mean, the way she's sorta squirmin', that's a sign, huh?"

"A man gets to know."

"Why'd Webster start this anyway?" Steve Grossett mumbled. "This isn't anything to bet about."

Cameron rolled over and stared at the sky, enjoying the growing warmth in his loins, wanting it to last, to grow slowly and firmly.

"Sid hates Adam Ward," he said. ". . . the way he runs this town, the way he almost fired my pa that time for orderin' through the Sears catalog."

"Folks is supposed to buy through the company store," Alfie responded sharply. "That's what it's for."

Quickly backing off the subject, Scott Cameron faced the house again. He lay on his belly, feeling his manhood grow strong beneath him.

At the pyracantha, the girl tilted her head to see the boy better.

"I can't even see your face," she was saying.

She moved around him, inspecting him.

"Of course, you're a soldier. My father was in the army. You're tall, aren't you?"

The soldier said something and she laughed, not at the words, for she didn't hear them, but at the tone. It pleased her. So gentle yet so masculine.

"I've never felt as comfortable with a boy before," she said.

His hand touched hers and she was surprised at how warm it felt. She hadn't known she was cold.

"Come," he said.

"Where?"

"Into the night."

She resisted. She told him "no" and meant it.

He insisted, urging her with the slightest pressure on her palm.

And they talked. She didn't know how long. It might have been a minute; it might have been an hour.

Then she was walking with him and it was right.

Toward the pond. They knew where they were going. Toward a gnarled tree, a star pine so twisted and bent by the seasons that it had escaped the saw that cut away the forest around it.

Behind them, beyond the ranges of their whispering voices, the men followed, crouched and running silently between shadows and shrubs.

Only Alfie's voice threatened to expose them. "He's gonna nail her," he bubbled. "Like a skin, he's gonna nail her right to the wall."

Scott Cameron smirked with pleasure. "Ward ain't gonna like that. A drifter makin' out with his daughter."

"Look at them," Alfie cried. "Will yuh look at 'em now."

From across the lake a fresh breeze rose, rippling the black glassy water and stirring the logs condemned to the saw. Reaching the gnarled tree, the wind whipped her skirts and tossed her sun-glow hair.

He held her lightly and they whirled, dancing, two moths around a hot and open flame. They kissed and their touch was as warm as the summer night, as untamed as the wind, as native as the uncut tree behind them.

"My gawd, he's touching her," Scott Cameron whimpered.

"Damn him," said Grossett.

"It's another sign, ain't it," said Alfie, and he inched forward, intrigued, trying to keep his hands above his waist, fearing the spot of moisture low on his belly. Not yet, he told himself. Please, just this once, not yet.

"I don't know; I don't understand," the girl said, but the hand on her breast comforted her, assured her.

Yet she resisted and yielded as the undecided wind cooled them and deserted them, until they slipped to the ground beside their tree.

"Not like this," she said, "I don't even know you."

But her writhing didn't stay his hands and his mouth never left her lips as he undressed her slowly, gently, as though he feared she'd shatter beneath his strength. When he had bared her to the waist, he kissed her there before dropping his fingertips to her still covered groin. He caressed her between the legs only enough to be sure she knew, then he helped her from the skirt, folding it beneath her as their only bed.

Poised above her, he stripped away the last vestige of cloth, then lowered himself until his manhood touched her gently in the soft vee of hair.

Deafened by the mutual groan of pleasure, blinded by eyes that shut out the world, neither saw the tall, slender figure stand above the brush only a few yards away.

"I'm going for Webster," Steve Grossett announced. "I'm going now."

At his feet Scott Cameron gaped. "What the hell for?"

"He's got to stop them. He can't let them do it. Not Catherine."

Grossett backed away and ran. Cameron stared after him, but Alfie didn't notice, for his body, belly down, was already convulsing, his organ protruding through his unzipped fly, its tip probing dirt.

From the group by the tree, Steve Grossett sprinted past the hedges, across the vacant lot and up the deserted street of buildings. A hundred yards from the store, he started to scream. "Mr. Webster, they're gonna do it. Honest to God, they are. You got to stop them."

"Wait a minute, Stephen," the old man soothed. "Calm your ass, boy."

"I can't," Grossett cried, his voice coming through between deep gasps for air. "That soldier, he's tearing her clothes off. He's touching her."

"Ain't been half hour."

"He's got her, by the pond. He's laying her. He said he would."

"Well, I'll be reamed. I wondered if he could. Saw his kind once before . . . in Tucumcari. Got a knack, some fellas. They can get a gal to spread her legs faster'n you and me can get 'em to say howdy."

"We ought to tell Ward," Grossett pleaded. "He'd stop them. He'd kill that soldier."

"Adam sure would."

"Let me tell him, please."

"Okay, Stephen, you tell Mr. Ward. You tell him his precious daughter is out there gettin' laid in the grass like a bitch dog."

"Thanks, Mr. Webster. Thanks a lot."

Webster corked the bottle and set it aside as he watched Grossett flee from the porch.

"Stephen, that you?" Ward demanded. "Why aren't you in your seat?"

"Mr. Ward, for gawd's sake, hurry. It's Catherine."

The glassine veneer around Adam Ward's eyes quivered and threatened to crack. "Catherine? She's inside."

"No. She's down by the pond. There's a man, a soldier . . . he's hurting her."

They rushed from the lobby together, out into the street to the black Cadillac parked directly in front. With Adam Ward at the wheel, Steve Grossett huddled against the opposite door.

"By the pond," Steve said, then said nothing more.

The car raced down the street and skidded into the driveway near the privet hedge. Together they leaped from the car.

But a hundred yards away near the pond the naked boy and the girl beneath him failed to hear the sound of slamming doors. Their lean bodies were coupled at the groin. Their hands cupped each other's buttocks. Their heads were turned aside, each fighting for breath, each moaning as if shocked at his own capability for pleasure.

Nearby Alfie Ward groaned too, although his hands were already smeared with sticky semen. "He's doin' it. He's doin' it."

Beside him, Scott Cameron stood for a better view. "Webster loses, sure as hell."

"Wish it was me out there," Alfie griped. "Damned sis. She'd never do nothin' like that with me. And me her own brother."

At the sound of crackling brush, Cameron turned, seeing the lights of the Cadillac.

"It's Steve," he called. "He's got your pa with him.

Alfie leaped to his feet. He tried to stuff his limp

penis back into his trousers, but he was still fumbling when Grossett and his father loomed before him.

"Where is she?" Ward demanded.

"There," Alfie pointed. "It's Catherine, Pa. She's dirty. I saw her. With a stranger. I saw her with my own eyes."

Ward shoved his son aside. With the others behind him, he plunged toward the naked couple.

On the ground the soldier heard the noise and reluctantly rolled away from the girl. He saw the shadows charging toward and he grabbed his clothes. "Time I left," he said as he clutched his trousers and shirt to his chest.

He paused to kiss the girl's cheek, but she pushed him aside and got to her feet. He heard her shouting, only he didn't understand at first. "Help!" she screamed. "Somebody help me. Please."

Panic knotted him to the spot. "Don't," he shook her. "They'll kill me."

He grabbed for her soft, bare shoulders, but she shook loose and went to meet the charging men. "Help, father! Stop him, please."

The soldier backed away. He held up his hand. He wanted to explain. He hadn't forced her. She had done it willingly, their bodies pounding together in a mutual demand for release.

But there was no time for explanations. The men were closing on him fast.

He broke and ran.

Naked, with his clothes clutched to his chest, he picked up momentum, the sound of their pounding footsteps just behind him. He plunged across the stream that fed the pond, cut towards the stacks of fallen trees near the mill, changed his mind at the sight of the lights, and darted through the cemetery of stumps toward the second growth in the distance.

At first he ran swiftly with the self-assurance of an animal, but as he crossed a logging road his bare feet were cut by sharp-edged stones. The stabbing pain broke his stride and his ankle twisted. Pain jabbed to his thigh and he let out a cry that his pursuers could hear.

Sensing his agony the pack behind pushed harder, baying after him with profanities and threats. Their breaths sounded like the snorting of huge, powerful animals, but his own came in short, frantic gasps.

They could feel his panic. He knew.

Still he plunged on blindly, deeper into the nightmare shadows of the darkened forest. Like the nails of invisible hands, brush lashed his flanks. Branches slapped his face. Then he fell. The earth seemed to fall away beneath his feet; he skidded across the decaying mat of pine needles on his shoulders.

Screaming, he slithered across the moist earth as the bizarre shadows of the men caught up with him and grasped for his flaying arms. He got up again, fell again and scrambled to his feet once more before an unseen hand knotted in his hair and dragged him back to the earth.

A booted foot kicked him in the stomach and he felt the vomit starting up his throat. Something hard and bony, a fist probably, battered his jaw. Something else hit him across the temple. Pain filled his chest cavity and he felt his nose flatten against his face.

He fought back, pounding his fists into the milling shadows above him, kicking too, even biting when a fist smashed his teeth. But it was hopeless.

Half-conscious he sank to his knees, then fell forward into the dirt. They were still kicking him when he vaguely heard an unfamiliar voice restraining the rest of his attackers.

He didn't move.

"Hold it," Adam Ward was saying. "He's not feeling anything more."

"Maybe he's dead," said another.

"Serves him right. Coming into town, rapin' sis like that. The bastard."

"I'll make sure he's dead," said a fourth voice.

Deep in his own private cavern of pain, the soldier knew the voice. It was the one they had called Grossett.

"No, leave him."

"But he raped your daughter."

"I said leave him. Go home. Forget him. And don't tell anybody what happened tonight. Nothing. Understand?" The others mumbled reluctant acceptance and backed away.

Then they were gone, all of them, and the soldier lay on the ground, his lungs still begging for breath, his body a weird crosswork of flaming agony and churning nausea. He had neither desire nor strength to move.

He had no idea how long he lay there. Time meant nothing to him.

Only the sound of crackling twigs aroused him. His fingers scratched earth and tried to pull him up, but his battered body collapsed again.

With effort he raised his head. Twin shadows stood ahead. A man's legs he guessed.

He tried to look higher, but his vision was blurred and distorted. He couldn't see the face.

He saw a knife, though. With its blade open and glistening in a shaft of moonlight, it hung from a hand along side one of the legs.

"Who are you?" the soldier asked with bloody lips. "I can't see."

Then a hand reached down and rolled him over onto his back.

"What are you doing?" he screamed with mounting terror.

He tried to rise but a heavy shoe pinned his wrist to the ground. The man above him knelt, driving a knee into the soldier's belly.

The soldier's broken fist pounded at the other man's back. Then he felt a cold hand at his groin and he understood.

"No! Damn you. No!"

He screamed.

He was still screaming long after the knife had sliced and cut. He was still screaming long after the other man had folded the blade and disappeared into the darkness.

Later when the soldier's screams had subsided to gagging agony, he blindly pressed his shorts between his legs to stop the bleeding and tried to stagger to his feet. He propped himself against a tree and cried like a child.

With blood streaming down his leg, he stumbled toward the highway, falling often but rising again and again with a curse on his lips.

Naked and vomiting, he staggered out of the woods and fell onto the pavement. He could see the lights of an approaching car, but he didn't care. It skidded to a stop inches from his head.

The driver popped out and came around the front. "Oh, gawd," he gasped. He knelt beside the bloody figure on the pavement and nearly retched. "I'll take you back to Timberland," he said finally. "Maybe there's a doctor there."

"No," the soldier groaned. "Not Timberland."

"But you're bleeding . . ."

"Not Timberland. Not now. Later."

"All right," the driver conceded, as he helped the soldier toward the car. "It's your blood you're spilling."

1972

CHAPTER 3

A twin-engine business jet dropped to the runway, slowed with a roar, and taxied across the small airport toward the stone and masonry administration building of Brannon Mills, Inc. From the window of the penthouse office Andrew Ledger looked down upon the aircraft.

A young man, not quite thirty, he carried his slender frame well, inside a carefully selected suit with fashionable lapels and a trim cut to the sides. A Negro with skin the color of lightly creamed coffee, he wore his hair short and kept a hint of a smile on his somewhat thick lips. His eyes, though, danced with real enthusiasm, and his hands worked briskly as he folded the last of the papers into the file he carried.

"Plane's in," he said. "Where's Brannon?"

He crossed the plushly furnished office to the built-in bar where the blonde finished mixing the drinks for the twin thermos bottles on the counter. Before she could pour from the shaker, he took it from her and filled a small glass for himself.

Marcia Hyde scowled at him. Five years his senior, she was as tall as he in her high-heeled shoes. Her skin was still fresh and unlined, and nothing about her severe business suit detracted from her sensually attractive face and body.

"*Mr.* Brannon is out in the mill," she chided.

He whacked her playfully on her girdled bottom and finished the drink. "Well, I'll find Brannon. You get his briefcase and meet us on the plane."

"There you go. Issuing orders again."

Grinning, he raised his clenched fist above his shoulder. "Black power," he said.

"Nigger," she told him.

But he was already through the door, passing her desk in the outer office and entering the carpeted hallway. He avoided the elevator and hurried down the cold metal stairway instead. At the second landing, his own secretary caught up with him and thrust another file into his hands.

"Leaving, Mr. Ledger?" she asked.

A pretty little black girl with a tremendous IQ, she invariably called him mister at the office, although they had slept together—occasionally—for more than a year.

"Soon as I find Brannon," he told her.

At the bottom of the stairway, he held the fire door for her and they went out into the plant. Cut into small empires by walkways painted onto the smooth cement floor, the huge building was a single, gigantic room under a steel-girdered roof. It hummed, clicked, and clacked.

Under the bored surveillance of human guards, machines stripped fresh paper from gargantuan rolls, then sliced it, printed it in simple lines and brilliant hues, folded and shaped it, and then spit it out on the far end of the form of boxes and napkins and sparkling containers. Tireless conveyor belts whisked it away toward the waiting trucks at the open doors of the shipping room.

But Andrew Ledger saw none of the products being born around him nor did he think of giant bleaching cells that bathed the color from the woodpulp. His flattened nose didn't even smell the stench of cooking sulfite. His mind was on the girl and the new thought she was throwing at him as they walked.

"Got something new on Timberland," she said.

"Not now. Brannon's due in Washington."

Ignoring him completely, she continued. "Looks like we'd better get control fast . . . if we hope to go through with the merger at all."

Ledger stopped and opened the file she had handed him on the stairs.

"The old man . . . Adam Ward," she said. "He's dying. Cirrhosis of the liver. He doesn't know it yet, but he hasn't much longer. Especially the way he drinks."

"The detectives dug that up for you?"

"Yes. They came across another little tidbit too. About the man named Webster."

"The one that disappeared. You found him?"

"No," she said. "But someone thought about checking social security."

"So?"

"Nothing. No receipts, no payments since 1953."

"Must be dead."

He folded the file and dismissed her. "Okay. I'll handle it. See you in a couple of days."

He left her and went out a side door. He passed

the mountains of wood chips that stretched along an elevated railway spur and walked between the towering cylinders of the digesters. His path took him beside the log-clogged river to the corrugated steel structure that quaked noticeably from the roar and vibration of the powerful cutting and chopping machines inside.

Within the building he clamped protectors over his ears and started up the metal ramps that led upward through the roaring, pounding blades and jaws of black steel. To his right, whole logs plummeted down a shaft into the razor-sharp teeth of a chipper. To his left, other logs rolled with a clattering thump into the slicing blades of a rotary saw.

At the end of one catwalk he stopped and shouted at the man who controlled the growling, clanking conveyor system. "Seen Brannon?" he asked.

There was no hearing amidst the sound of metal arms tossing huge logs about like twigs, but the man read his lips and shouted back. "Try the barker. He goes in there sometimes."

Following the suggestion, he climbed a metal stair, crossed an open grating and went through a steel door into the dimly-lit control room of the hydraulic debarker. The man sitting at the aircraft-like panel didn't look back. His eyes were trained through the thick glass wall ahead of him. Beyond the protective glass, logs fresh from the river crashed downward onto a platform of turning cogwheels. As the log spun on the wheels, an arm stretched downward from the ceiling. High-powered jets of water sprayed from the arm, blasting the bark away in a holocaust of driven rain and flying chips.

Against the background roar, Ledger had to get

his face in front of the man where he could read his lips. "Seen Brannon?" he asked.

"By the crane," the man responded, without looking away from the next log that rolled into position for stripping.

Ledger nodded and went back outside.

Taking another catwalk, he moved to the open bay where an overhead crane dipped two finger-like prongs into the river below. Grasping nearly fifty tons of logs with its thumbs and forefingers, the machine hoisted them several stories out of the water with a powerful, contented roar. With a shattering rumble that shook the entire building, the mammoth bundle crunched to the platform at the beginning of the conveyor system.

Just beyond the end of the logs stood Brannon.

Lean and tall, his body appeared powerful even under the white shirt and the stiffly pressed trousers of his expensive suit. His hair was dark and full, with a hint of gray at the temple. His face was handsome but a little stern, a suggestion of anger given it by the faint scar high on his cheek just below his left eye. His lips, though, smiled when he saw the Negro approaching.

"Brannon," Ledger called. "Plane's here."

The white man looked back down at the clipboard in his hands and made another mark, seeming to ignore the imploring call of his assistant.

"We'll just make the hearing," Ledger coaxed.

In front of them a workman stepped out to cut the metal straps that held the bundle of logs together. When the logs had rolled loose, Brannon passed the clipboard to the other man.

Ledger trailed after him down the catwalk. He

called out even though he knew it was nearly impossible to be heard. "I got something new on Timberland, too, boss."

Brannon stopped abruptly and took the file from his assistant's hand. Eagerly he opened it. "Adam Ward . . . he's dying . . . and that man named Webster, the one you asked about so often, apparently he's already dead."

Brannon quickly read the reports inside the file, then folded it and passed it back to Ledger. Together they walked to the nearest exit. In the bright warmth of the summer afternoon, they headed toward the side gate that opened onto the airport.

"That new jet—can it set down at Timberland?" Brannon asked abruptly.

Ledger scowled at the unexpected question. "At Chestertown. That's as close as we can get. But what about Washington? There's twenty thousand acres of Douglas fir involved."

"Screw Washington." Brannon spit out the last words like a curse and stalked away toward the plane.

Stunned, Andrew Ledger stared after his boss as if he had never seen the man before.

Inside the jet, Marcia Hyde came out of the pilot's cockpit and walked up the narrow aisle to the lap desk where Andrew Ledger and Brannon bent over a sheath of papers.

". . . a California corporation," Ledger was saying. "Originally capitalized at five million dollars with headquarters, lumber mill, and timber holdings within a twelve mile radius . . ."

"Still no hotel in Timberland," Marcia interrupted.

Brannon looked up at her with apparent interest.

"I've booked us a place on the lake outside of town," she said.

As she took the nearest seat, Brannon switched his attention to the window. He stared down on the green carpet of the tree farms that extended to the horizon in every direction.

"Want the pilot to circle Timberland?" Ledger asked.

"There's not much to see," said Marcia. "A virtual ghost town. Dying slowly, like an animal bleeding to death from a small wound. That's how the paper described it once."

"Nothing left of the lumber mill," Ledger reminded him. "Foundations, a few crumbling walls, everything else went for scrap. I can't imagine what you think we're getting for our money. Timberland's been practically deserted since the early fifties."

Brannon kept his back to them as he answered. "I'm buying a town and everybody in it."

Ledger's black face twisted impatiently. "But there's nobody there . . . nobody who counts. A company town after the mill closed . . . a few old people . . . a couple of ex-loggers scratching a living from cut-over land . . . a storekeeper or two . . . nobody we can use."

Brannon faced them slowly. "There's a whole family of Wards. Maybe we can use them."

Ledger wrinkled his brow to show his puzzlement. "Yes, Adam Ward . . . the old patriarch. A daughter, a son-in-law, a grandchild too."

"And a son," Brannon corrected.

Confused, Marcia took a file from the desk and thumbed far back into its papers. "Alfred," she said. "He's in his forties now. A half-wit. A child in a man's body."

"That's the one," Brannon said. "Alfie. Good old Alfie."

"You knew him?" Ledger asked. "I thought you'd never been to Timberland. I thought. . . ."

Brannon turned his head back to the window.

"Have a car standing by at the airport. I want to go straight into Timberland."

"It'll be dark by then. If we went out to the lake instead, we could call Washington."

Brannon's voice came back muffled. His tone was cold and foreign, a tone they hadn't heard before. "Washington can wait. But not Alfie. I've waited long enough for him."

CHAPTER 4

Alfie Ward—his hair scraggly and thin, his shoulders stooped and bony, but his eyes wild and alive.

He yanked the frayed cord that hung from the ceiling of the open cab and giggled when the whistle gasped one weak and final toot. He pulled the cord several times more. Nothing. But he didn't care. He could always make the tooting sound with his mouth. And he did, repeatedly until he swung down out of the cab.

"Train's in, folks," he announced. "All aboard."

In the light from his lantern, the station ahead was a dark shell. The main door hung loose from a single hinge. The windows were black with accumulated dirt. A few were shattered, sharp petals of glass blooming from their hollow centers.

"Train's in," he said again.

Then he crossed the rotting and splintered ramp and stuck his head inside the empty waiting room. He held his lamp high and swung it back and forth, momentarily enjoying the pendulum shadows it created. Except for the single bench the room was gutted of furnishings and the floor was sagged and warped.

Alfie sighed. No passengers. Oh, well.

He left the station and shuffled across the tracks toward the street of stores.

In the center of the street, he paused. A light wind swirled the dust around him and launched a few scraps of paper upward on a brief flight from the gutter.

With the exception of a single light from the grocery window and another above the filling station, the street was dark. On either side of him the buildings were black, angular shadows—some with broken roof lines where unmelted snow had crushed the peaks.

At the far end of the street, the gray hulk of the auditorium still stood. Across from it was the theater and farther on the gutted charcoal remains of the church, its scarred timbers exposed to the late evening sky.

Only one vehicle parked along the curb. A rusted pickup truck, its right front tire was flat.

To be sure nothing had changed since morning, Alfie raised his lantern to shoulder height and peered underneath it. Then he went over to the store and swung open the screen.

"Train's in," he called. "Got any passengers?"

Behind the counter, Scott Cameron looked over his shoulder sharply. When he saw it was Alfie, he ducked his head again.

Alfie had to come around the cash register to see what was happening.

He recognized Alma. Her fleshy hips were pressed back against the sparse display of breakfast food and the front of her house dress was spread wide open. Cameron was ardently kissing her sagging breasts.

"What the hell," she said, brushing a hand back through her stringy hair.

She shoved Cameron away and waddled from behind the counter. She extended her tongue at Alfie and disappeared through the door.

"Watcha doin' with her?" Alfie asked. "Pickin' fleas?"

Cameron wiped a hand across his mouth and straightened his smudged white hair with his arthritic hand. "I was fittin' her for a brassiere, you stupid loghead. It's my job."

"Betcha'd like to fit her for bloomers too."

Cameron elbowed Alfie out of the way and went to the door. "Wait, Alma," he called. "I'll bring some beer." He went back to the cooler and began ripping cans from a six pack.

"She's uglier than possum, that Alma."

Cameron grunted agreement. "A shepherd takes on the prettiest sheep in the flock. What else can he do? Watch the store 'til I get back."

"Don't go," Alfie pleaded. "Come on down to the station with me. You can toot my whistle. I got her workin' again."

"I'd rather toot hers."

Alfie followed him out onto the street and stared after him until he disappeared around the corner.

"Damn," the half-wit swore. "He ain't no fun. Nobody ain't no fun no more."

He settled into the rocking chair on the porch and propped his feet against the upright pillar to the tilted roof. Carefully he looked along the street, reassuring himself with the familiarity of the shadowy buildings and the few distant lights. To his left he could see the faint glow in the windows of the big house beyond the broken hedge, and in the upper story of the frame apartment in the next block, he could see the yellow lamp in the old preacher's bedroom.

The wind whistled softly and he twisted in his chair. A door rattled somewhere and he thought he heard footsteps coming up behind him.

He shivered. But he wasn't afraid, he told himself. He wasn't alone. There were still lots of people in town, dozens at least.

Then he lurched at a sudden movement on the edge of his vision. He almost cried out before he recognized the black mongrel dog padding aimlessly along the edge of the street.

Just inside the light from the store window, the dog stopped. He stared at Alfie.

Alfie leaned forward over the rail of the porch. He spat, missing the dog by inches.

Indignantly, the dog barked. He came a step closer, yapping louder.

Finding a rusted beer can beneath the chair, Alfie heaved it over the railing. The metal edge cracked the animal on the flanks, but he stood his ground, barking angrily until Alfie found another missile.

The dog retreated reluctantly, pausing again in the shadows. He barked one more rebuke and then was gone.

Satisfied, Alfie rolled back in his chair.

He was rocking contentedly when the lights of a panel truck turned onto the street. The truck parked directly in front of the store and an old man got out.

"You minding the store, Alfie?" he asked.

"Yep."

"Can I get some things? Cigarettes, mainly."

Alfie conjured up his most important pose and answered with regal indifference. "Leave the money on the counter."

The old man went inside and Alfie resumed rocking.

He stopped again when a year-old sedan turned the corner street and stopped beside the truck.

Stephen Grossett leaned out the window and called to Alfie. "You see Cameron?"

"Naw," Alfie lied.

He always lied to his brother-in-law. The man was too neat, too well dressed, like he had a real job or something. And his hair, so full and black when most men his age were bald or maybe gray at least.

"Naw," he said again. "I ain't seen him."

Behind him, the old man came out of the store. "Evening, Dr. Grossett," he said pleasantly.

As the old man walked to the panel truck, Grossett mumbled a reply, then spoke again to Alfie. "Find Cameron," he ordered. "Get him over to the house. We've got troubles."

"Yeah, sure," Alfie agreed. "Right away."

But as the vehicles pulled away, he leaned back in the chair and closed his eyes smugly.

He'd beat that Grossett guy again. College men. What'd they know anyway? Nothing.

He giggled to himself and put his hands between his legs. He felt warm and comfortable and sleep came easily.

If he dreamed, he didn't know, and he came awake slowly to the sound of a motor rumbling nearby. He sat stiffly upright when he realized a car, an unfamiliar one, already sat across the street. Its perfectly tuned engine idled softly and in its dark interior he could make out the shadows of people.

Strangers!

Alfie gasped and wanted to cry. He was afraid. Alone on a deserted street with a dark and unfamiliar car parked so menacingly near.

"Cameron," he cried out. "Hey, Cameron! Where the hell are you?"

He got to his feet and held his lantern at shoulder height, but its light fell distressingly short of the shadowed car. He felt the palms of his hands perspire and he feared he'd wet his pants. He did that sometimes when he was afraid.

"Who's that out there?" he called.

Forcing himself from the porch, he stepped into the street.

The car door opened and Alfie almost stumbled over his own feet.

"Pa!" he called hopefully. "Hey, Pa."

The figure from the car was a huge—big, black and lumbering like a bear. Alfie held the lantern high again and the light cut the shadow down to man-size. Still, Alfie's hand shook and his eyes watered.

He wanted to run, but he was afraid to turn his back on the figure as it came steadily closer.

"Hello, Alfie," the figure said in a strange and hollow voice.

Alfie quivered at the sound of his own name. How did the shadow know him so well.

The face of the man came into the light and Alfie whimpered.

The face was stern, almost parental, and there was

a small scar high on the man's cheek just below the left eye.

Alfie had never seen the face before. At least he couldn't remember. But the stranger had called him by name.

"I don't know you," he whined. "How'd you know my name."

"Been a long time, Alfie. Don't you remember?"

Alfie retreated a step and looked about for an escape route. "I never seen you before, not in my whole life."

"Sure you did, Alfie. Just think back, boy. You'll remember."

The lantern slipped from Alfie's hand and he stumbled back along the wooden walk. "Get away from me," he screamed. "Don't touch me. I didn't do nothin'. Cross my heart, I didn't."

The man from the car picked up the lantern and it streaked his dark suit and stern face with flared wedges of light.

Alfie floundered. He bumped against the cracked, candy-cane pole of the old barber shop and fled past the shattered window of the long vacant pool hall. When his foot twisted in the rotted planking, he fell to his knees before the ghostly figure that trailed him by only a dozen paces.

He was screaming. He knew that, but the street was whirling around him. He could hear the man from the car calling to someone else; he could hear another man's voice; but he couldn't understand why the light kept coming closer, ever closer.

He got up again and ran, his feet like leaden weights that flopped uncontrollably at the end of his wobbly legs. His arms flayed the air and his head flopped from side to side. He couldn't see anymore. He wasn't even sure why he was running.

Finding the boarded doors of the auditorium almost by accident, he smashed against them with his shoulder until the rusted nails gave under his weight. He fell forward into the mirrored lobby and screamed at the sight of his own image reflected back at him through the grime-covered glass.

At the sound of footsteps outside, he scrambled through the inner doors and found himself completely blinded in the unlighted auditorium. Soft, hairlike fingers caressed his face and hard, unyielding boards cracked at his ankles.

He lashed out with his hands, but the thick, invisible webs snarled his fingers, and his body seemed to come alive with crawling, slithering things that only his imagination could visualize.

He was screaming wildly by the time the man with the lantern came through the doors and held the light high enough to probe the crumbling dance floor with its folding chairs still in rigid rows and its dust-covered piano still waiting for the forgotten touch of a human hand.

"Get outa here," Alfie cried toward the light. "Pa don't 'low nobody in here. Everybody knows that."

"Why?" the voice asked. "How come its closed? The whole town . . . the mill, the theater, the bunkhouses. How come, Alfie?"

"I don't know. It's always been like this."

"No, it hasn't. Don't you remember? Twenty years ago. Music. A woman singing."

Alfie heard sounds deep inside his head. Music. A woman's voice. A piano.

He saw lights too, a glittering, sparkling thing that hung from the ceiling and sprayed the floor below with little colored squares.

People. He remembered people too, so many they crowded the whole floor of the auditorium or filled the pews of the church. The theater too. He remembered that. Snow White, where had she gone?

"Mama," he called out, and he couldn't remember why. "Mama," he said again.

Then he cupped his hands over his ears and stepped back into the darkness. He couldn't remember where he was. A closet, maybe. He was being punished. That was it. They did that sometimes . . . put him in the closet when people were coming.

"Sit there and be quiet," they'd tell him. "Sit there and don't say a word 'til they're gone."

He sat on the edge of the wooden stage, folded his arms around his knees and laid his head down between them.

He no longer heard the man behind the lantern. He didn't even feel the frayed side curtain as it crumpled at the touch of his shoulder and fell around him like ashes from a broken mantle.

CHAPTER 5

Brannon said no more. He stood above the hunched figure on the stage for a time, trying to understand his own emotions. Was it hate, he wondered? Or anger? Or perhaps even envy. He almost laughed aloud. Envy . . . of a befuddled half-wit who hunched into the ball shape of a fetus? Could anyone envy such a lump of flesh?

He could.

With the thought came rage. His eyes smarted and the veins in his temples throbbed. The muscles in his fingers tightened. He felt the stiff wire handle of the lantern more intently and realized he had a weapon, a club for cracking a skull.

But then he heard the doors creaking open at the front of the auditorium. He turned, but he couldn't make out the figure coming down the aisle through the darkness.

"Brannon, that you?" Andrew Ledger asked.

The black man picked his way down the aisle until he stood beside Brannon on the stage. He looked down at Alfie. "You know him?"

Brannon moved off the stage, leaving the inert lump of flesh behind, before he answered. "He didn't remember me," he said.

Ledger caught up with him in the lobby. He

caught him by the arm and tried to hold him back.

"Then you have been here before?" Ledger asked.

But again his boss ignored him.

They walked out into the street and down past the deserted pool-hall toward the Mercedes. Before they reached it, Brannon's secretary slipped out of the back seat and stood waiting.

She wore a coat, though the night was warm, but she shivered noticeably. Her eyes were wide with fright; she hugged herself for reassurance.

Brannon understood. She had never been alone before—not in the center of a town with dead, vacant buildings standing around her like huge and foreboding grave stones.

"Boss," Ledger asked as they reached the car. "What the hell are we doing here?"

Brannon didn't answer, but he put a reassuring hand on Marcia's shoulder.

"Are you all right?" she asked him. He had to smile at her concern.

"Of course," he told her. "You wait here. Then pick me up in front of the Ward house in ten minutes. It's the big place at the end of the street. You can't miss it."

"You sure you want to be alone in this town?" Ledger wondered. "I don't like it."

Brannon looked about him, seeing the dark, angular shadows through their eyes and hearing the night sounds with their ears. The mournful wind, the rustle of the trees like a woman's skirts, the distant yap of a dog, a creaking door. A movement at the edge of your vision. And always the feeling of aloneness as though help would always be just a little too far away.

They were afraid.

And well they should be. Once recognized, the town would want them dead, all of them.

"Damn," Ledger said suddenly. "You got to give us some idea what we're doing in this graveyard."

"Buying a town," Brannon answered.

"A ghost town," Marcia added.

"But why, Brannon? You don't buy company shells or run off on hair-brained ideas. "You're all business."

"Of course."

"Then what's here that you could want?"

Brannon stooped and set the lantern on the warped boards of the walk beside the car.

"You'll see," he said; then he left them and started up the street in the direction he remembered.

Behind him he could hear Ledger still puzzling with the problem.

"I don't understand. What the hell could he want in Timberland?"

"A woman," Marcia answered.

"A woman?" he heard Ledger's fading voice respond. "Maybe you're right."

From the car, Brannon walked through the darkness until he approached the scraggly, dying remnants of a privet hedge. Beyond the hedge he could see the lights of a house, but he veered to the left and found the reed-choked pond.

Taxing his memory, he sought out the gnarled tree he remembered. In his mind he could recall its ugly, twisted shape, yet in the darkness he floundered, wandering helplessly until a single point of light flared directly ahead of him. He moved closer and saw a twisted limb silhouetted against the navy blue of the night sky.

He felt excitement and a deep sense of pleasure he hadn't permitted himself in years. It was the tree, the same bent and broken tree he remembered from before.

Then he saw the light again and with it the faint hint of a figure.

He approached cautiously until he recognized the vague shape of a woman.

He stopped, suddenly unsure of his own bodily reactions. His heart was pounding hard as though he had been running for blocks. He was breathing fast, and he felt a demanding urge to back away.

Ridiculous, he told himself. Stupid.

But there was a slight note of hope in his voice as he called out, almost in a whisper. "Catherine?"

The light by the tree fell to the ground and the figure retreated toward the house.

He didn't follow. Instead he stepped up under the gnarled limbs. Around him the night wind grew abruptly angry, tousling his hair and slapping at his face. It shoved at his chest as though to push him away, and its voice was almost human in its anguish. He even whirled to be sure he was still alone. But there was only the wind and the restless leaves of the tree.

Seeing a spark at his feet, Brannon stooped and pushed the butt of a cigarette with his finger. He felt better, knowing he hadn't imagined the figure he had seen a moment before.

He ground out the cigarette and then headed in the direction of the house.

He had no plans. He knew he wouldn't go inside.

Not yet. Not tonight. Later perhaps, but now he just wanted to probe, to find the pyracantha, to see the porch where they had stood. He asked for nothing more.

His memory served him well and he moved easily across the open field to the yard. But the moon surprised him as it cast a bright shaft of light across the area he remembered as a flowered garden.

Nothing bloomed in spite of the season. Weeds and leafless stalks populated the bare spots around the grassy patches. Bushes were flat and sagging as though untrimmed in years. Dandelions pushed through all the cracks in the walks, and a small gazebo sagged under the weight of a dead and snarled vine.

Across the yard, though, he caught the sight of a movement, a wisp of white, like smoke rising on a windless day.

It was a woman, the same one he had seen at the tree, only clearer now in the moonlight.

She appeared to float, whirling slowly as though she danced in a dream. The skirt of her frock lifted and fell in slow motion. Her arms rose in a gentle wave, and her long blonde hair broke loose from the knot at the back and fell around her shoulders.

Brannon moved closer to convince himself. There was no pleasure in the woman's dance, only a deep, lonely sorrow.

The figure made one last whirl, then stopped abruptly as the woman saw him standing there in the shadows.

The moonlight washed across her face and he saw the startled expression sweep away the dreamy loneliness he had detected in her movements.

Oh!" she said.

He recognized her at once. The years had been kind. Her hair was still soft and gently curled. Her flesh was still unblemished. Her mouth was older, but still full and curved, the kind a man likes to kiss, her high cheekbones were still arched and proud.

He couldn't tell about her eyes. He imagined a sadness that he might not have seen in a better light.

Her figure, too, he had to imagine, but it seemed fuller around the breasts than he recalled. The waist, though, was still slender and her legs beneath the skirt were none the worse for age.

"Steve?" she asked. "Is that you?"

The voice changed. The tone was the same, so was the timbre, but the last lingering hint of childhood was gone. She was a woman, not the girl he remembered.

Yet he couldn't resist the urge to step so close that their bodies almost touched.

Strangely she didn't pull back in fright, not even when he put his hand to her neck and ran his fingers into her hair.

But as his hand fell away, she stepped back as though she had been stung.

"You're not Steve," she said. "Who are you?"

"The name is Brannon," he told her.

"Brannon?"

With his hands trembling, he reached in his pocket for a cigarette. He held one out to her and she took it. He smoked infrequently, but he needed the delay now until he could be certain of his voice again.

"You're Catherine Ward, aren't you?" he said when he was sure of himself again.

"Grossett. Mrs. Catherine Grossett."

"Oh, yes, I'd forgotten. You're married."

She shifted positions, trying to get the moonlight to his face, but he carefully kept his features in the shadows. She wouldn't recognize him, he knew that, not after all the years in between, not with a name different from the one he had given her that night, but he didn't want to take a chance either. Not yet. There'd come a time when they'd all remember him. When he was ready. But now.

"And you're *that* Mr. Brannon," she said.

"You know me?"

"I know the name. We learned recently that you're the one who has been buying Ward Timber Company stock through street names for several years. You're our only buyer, I might add. But won't you come in? My husband and the others, they're meeting . . . about you, in fact."

She started for the door, but stopped when he didn't follow.

"Not just now," he told her. "They'd want to discuss the firm."

"And you already have all the information you need, I suppose?"

"I have enough."

"I know. Income tax records, list of stockholders, all the confidential data on our sick little company." She paused thoughtfully. "We'll fire the man who provided it to you, of course."

"You already did, a year ago, like virtually all your other employees. Lately we've had to use private detectives."

She tipped her head and seemed to be considering

him more seriously now. "You came to buy us, Mr. Brannon. Is that correct?"

"Are you for sale?"

She caught the innuendo and her voice came back curt and sharp. "Nothing is for sale in Timberland. Not to you."

"No hotel, no U.S.O., no place for a stranger," he mused.

"What?"

"There's no hotel. I had to sublet a place at the lake."

"Oh," she said.

He considered her carefully, then plunged ahead with the first thought that entered his mind. "Join me," he suggested, "at the lake."

"I beg your pardon."

". . . for a dip and a drink. It's a perfect night."

"Really, Mr. Brannon, my husband insists I. . . ."

"I'm not inviting your husband," he interrupted. Before she could answer, the lights of the Mercedes swept toward the house. The motor rumbled softly at the curb, and Catherine climbed the steps to the porch. "Good night, Mr. Brannon. Perhaps, tomorrow you'll join us."

The screen door slammed behind her, and Brannon stood alone at the foot of the steps.

"Tomorrow?" he said aloud to himself. "I'll have you naked by then, you and your whole damned town."

The wind came up strong. It shook the squat bushes and bent the dried stalks of dead flowers. And when he headed toward his car, the wind dried the moisture in Brannon's eyes.

CHAPTER 6

Entering the house, Catherine looked critically at the furnishings for the first time in years. Everything was old—even the wallpaper—and dark. She particularly hated the hallway. The light had burned out months before and no one had replaced it. And the open staircase to the upper floor—new carpeting should have been laid long ago.

She was glad Brannon hadn't accepted her invitation. Perhaps the house wouldn't look quite so bad in the daylight.

But as she went into the living room with its tall cathedral ceiling and its massive fireplace, she knew daylight wouldn't help. The couch, the leather chairs, the mahogany end tables . . . everything in the room was old. Her mother's. She and Steve had changed little since they had moved in with her father.

At the side of the fireplace, her husband stood. He was still a handsome man, having gained none of the excess weight which plagues so many men his age. But as usual his face was sober and rigid. He didn't even speak when she entered. He never did.

To Steve's right at the built-in bar, the only recent addition to the room, her father was pouring from a bourbon bottle. He used a small glass. He always did as if he intended to drink only a few swallows of the amber liquid.

Not that it mattered much. She had seen the last doctor's report. Her father hadn't long to live, a condition she found neither appalling nor particularly interesting. It just didn't seem to matter.

"No, it just says Brannon appeared in Los Angeles in the fifties," her husband was saying, "apparently with several thousand dollars."

Catherine saw the file in her husband's hand and recognized it as their latest report.

". . . moved into a rented room," Steve continued.

". . . and immediately invested in the stock market," Catherine contributed from memory.

Her husband shook his head and ran his finger down the file until he found what he was looking for, ". . . commodity market actually. Rather daring for a nineteen-year-old boy. He hit it big in soybeans . . . pyramiding until the brokers got nervous."

"Then switched to lumber."

"Paper, to be precise. He saw the boom coming in computers and was there to feed them the paper they eat up so fast."

"So what does he want with us?" Adam Ward's fragile old voice asked sharply from the bar. "What the hell does he want with us?"

"I can't imagine," Catherine said, as she fixed herself a drink.

Her father buried his nose in his drink and mumbled to himself when he came up for air. "If we could only stall. Maybe we could get a loan, buy back some of the stock, enough to guarantee control again."

She sensed the terror in his voice, but his weakness angered her, and she wanted to slap him across the face as one might slap a spoiled child who's wallowing in self-pity. Instead she spoke matter-of-factly to her husband. "Didn't those investigators we hired dig up anything interesting on Brannon? Anything personal? What about women? Is he married?"

"No. No hobbies either. Nothing but an all-consuming passion to amass a fortune. He operates mainly through an assistant—an Andrew Ledger—and a secretary." He paused, scanning something he had found earlier in the file. "Oh, here's something else. Brannon conducts most business at night, displaying a propensity for dim or unlighted rooms."

The terror in Adam Ward's voice mounted again. "Unlighted rooms? What kind of a maniac are we dealing with?"

Steve Grossett searched the report again. "Evidently his face is scarred. Only slightly, nothing very disfiguring."

Catherine held her drink aside and thought about the scars. She had noticed nothing like that when she had talked to Brannon a moment before, but then she had seen little of his face.

"Scars?" she said. "Now that's something I can use."

"How?" her father asked.

"I'm a woman. Have you forgotten, father?"

Adam Ward shuffled across the room and slumped into a chair. "You bore a child. I guess that's proof."

Catherine ignored the sarcasm and thought of Brannon, the strange man who had run his fingers through her hair even before they had spoken.

"He's obviously shy," she said. "Conscious of his scars, probably."

Her father put his drink aside and scowled at her critically. "Catherine, you ought to leave this to me."

His tone cut her. She'd heard it before, the same tone whenever she had mentioned a man, any man.

"Really, father," she said, her voice sugary sweet yet filled with contempt. "Were you planning to be sober?" She put her drink on the bar and walked to the staircase, pausing for effect. "That would be nice, wouldn't it? Such a refreshing change."

She started up the stairs, then twirled on them, and shouted back at them like children. "Idiots. Stupid weak idiots. If I hadn't listened to you fools, there wouldn't be a man named Brannon, a man we don't even know. Right under your noses, he accumulates forty-eight percent of our company . . . our town . . . our whole lives. So curl up in a chair and suck your thumbs. I don't give a damn."

"You bitch," her father cursed.

She turned her back on him and continued up the stairs, but she could hear him shouting at Steve. "You shouldn't let her talk that way. You're her husband."

"It doesn't matter," Steve's voice said weakly. "It's never mattered."

At the top of the stairs, she waited, listening to them, enjoying their misery.

"She wasn't always like this, was she?" her father asked. "Sometimes I can't recall."

Her husband mumbled something more, but the sound of the door chimes blocked the words.

Standing back out of sight, she waited until she heard her husband opening the door.

"Where've you been," she heard him say to someone. "I sent for you hours ago."

The next voice was Scott Cameron's and it sounded almost as frightened as her father's. "It's Alfie," he said. "He's at it again."

She could hear her father come stumbling out of the living room and she shared the weakness she knew he felt. "Alfie, he's searching again."

Adam Ward choked. "Oh, gawd. Where this time?"

"At the mill," Scott Cameron answered. "You want me to bring him in alone?"

"No. He's my son."

She heard the door slam, and she felt a wave of guilt sweep over her. She knew what Alfie's rages did to her father, and she had added to his misery with her own outburst.

Damn, she said to herself. Damn that Alfie.

Leaving the top of the stairs, she stopped at the first open door. Looking in, she saw her daughter standing at the window.

"Louise, please, come away from there," she said.

But as she entered the unlit room, her daughter stayed at the window, her lithe young body softly illuminated in the moonlight.

With hair the color of her mother's and a sweet gentle face, she seemed like something from an earlier, simpler age, yet she had graduated from high school with honors and skipped college only by choice. And since then she had spent much of her time here in her room, all too often looking out into the night as though searching for something she could never have.

"Mother, look. Over there," she said, and she pointed through the window into the distance. "You can see his lantern."

At the window Catherine too could see the small cone of light near the crumbling buildings of the old mill. She could see movement too, and she remembered the first time she had seen her brother on a rampage.

He had always been slow. She had learned to live with that, but the searching, that was insane. She had seen his eyes suddenly grow glazed and his mouth hang open as though the jaw muscles had lost their strength. Spit dripped from his mouth and urine stained his pant leg. With his arms and head flopping, he had run up and down the deserted streets of the town, smashing his way into one building after another. They had caught up with him eventually in one of the empty bunkhouses. He had thrown himself on the floor and ripped away the linoleum. With his bare, bleeding hands, he was trying to tear up the heavy planking beneath.

"Why does he do it? Why, mother?" Louise pleaded as she turned from the window, her face lined with a panic of her own. "What is he searching for . . . all these years?"

"He doesn't even know himself, dear."

"Then stop him," Louise screamed. "Stop him from digging in the earth and tearing out the walls like a madman." She pressed her face against her mother's shoulder; Catherine could feel her sobbing.

Looking above her toward the mill, Catherine could see the figures of the men as they reached the lantern. They'd talk to him now, her father and

Cameron. In soft, gentle voices they'd reassure him while he grunted like a pig and rooted in the ground with his fingers. Later, when he had spent his imagined rage, they'd bring him in, weeping and bathed in sweat.

"It's all right, dear" Catherine assured her daughter. "Your grandfather will quiet him soon."

She eased the girl to the bed, and they sat together on the edge.

Louise sobbed. "But it'll happen again. A cross word from someone . . . a stranger in town . . . and he'll go wild like that . . . ripping the walls from an empty building, digging in the ground with his fingers. Searching, always searching."

"He doesn't hurt anyone, not really."

Louise raised her head. "Will you say that about me?" she asked.

"What?"

"When I'm like him . . . when I've lost my mind too, will you let me wander the streets? Will you buy me my own engine, my own whistle?"

Catherine clutched her closer. "What are you saying? You're not like him."

"We have the same blood."

"That doesn't mean. . . ."

"A madman for an uncle . . . a grandmother who deliberately walks in front of a truck. . . ."

"Alfred's not mad," Catherine said quickly. "Retarded, yes, but not mad."

"Then what about you?" her daughter asked accusingly.

"Me?"

Louise leaped up and went back to the window.

She pointed off to the right, toward the pond and the gnarled tree.

"Standing out there, every night, alone. What are you looking for . . . waiting for? A man?"

Catherine left the bed and stood beside her daughter. There the moonlight played tricks with her face, as her expression flitted from hope to depression and on to desperation.

She spoke, more to herself that to her daughter. "A man? What kind of man, dear?"

When her daughter didn't answer, Catherine folded her arms across her middle, then ran her hands gently up over her breasts.

"A young man," she mumbled, "with strong arms and dark hair and the smell of beer on his breath."

Her voice faded and was still as the dying night wind beyond the window.

CHAPTER 7

Brannon raised the beer can and drank the last of the cold, biting liquid. He didn't particularly like the taste, but it seemed appropriate at the moment.

The wind had died now and from the porch of his rented house he looked out over the still lake that claimed a few hundred acres of the pine forest for itself. Only a dozen lights dotted the shoreline. Even so the lake seemed so much more alive than Timberland, just six or seven miles away through the trees.

And he felt safer here.

Yet he lurched at the sound of a sliding door opening behind him.

Marcia came out carrying a small reel of amateur movie film that she held up for emphasis. "I have the projector set up in the study," she said. "Or would you prefer to watch it out here."

"No," he said.

As he passed her going into the house, she took the empty can from his hand and dropped it in a waste basket just inside the plushly furnished living room. She'd want the room neat, he knew. No beer cans or empty drink glasses left on the Dutch colonial tables, no cigarette butts left for long in the ceramic ashtrays.

Almost for spite he went to the standup bar and

took another beer from the ice chest. He opened the pop-up top and left the ring on the counter top where she'd have to police it.

On the stairs above him, he saw Andrew Ledger scowling. "I thought you said beer was a nigger's drink?" the black man said.

Brannon agreed, then led the way into the adjoining study with its wall cases of secondhand books and its gas-fed flames in the floor-to-ceiling fireplace.

A glass-bead screen on a tripod was already set up, and Marcia had carefully arranged several chairs at a comfortable distance. While he and Ledger settled into the chairs, she fed the reel of film into the machine.

She switched off the lights and tried to focus the picture onto the screen.

The scene before them remained blurred and poorly lit. Obviously it had been shot by an amateur who had difficulty with the complicated telephoto lens.

"He was shooting through the window into the living room," Marcia began. She raised her hand then and pointed to the unsteady figure entering the corner of the screen. "That's Adam Ward, Chairman of the Board."

"Big title for a defunct company," Ledger added sarcastically.

"Two hundred thousand shares," she continued. "No longer active. And he's drinking himself to death. Doesn't seem to care . . . except maybe for his grandfather. He's particularly partial to her."

On the screen the figure of Catherine Grossett appeared briefly and Brannon leaned forward in his chair. Even as he made the movement, he sensed the slight turn of Marcia's head. She was perceptive, too perceptive sometimes.

"Catherine Ward Grossett," Ledger commented. "One hundred thousand shares. Director. No other official title."

"But she runs what is left of the family empire," Marcia contributed, "with the cold efficiency of a red-light madam." She hesitated as the screen faded to black, then bloomed again with a picture of Steve Grossett climbing into his car. "Her husband," Brannon heard her say, but she seemed to be speaking from a distance.

Steve Grossett. The man hadn't changed, Brannon thought bitterly. That was one face he would remember anywhere.

"Doctor," Marcia was saying. "Small practice. Titular president of the company. Does exactly as he's told. But he has forty thousand shares in his own name."

Again the image on the screen flickered off. A second later the lens came back into focus and spread before them in life size was the naked figure of a girl. In her late teens, Brannon figured quickly, nicely shaped, although a little on the thin side. She lay on her stomach on a multi-colored serape, evidently soaking up the sun.

"Whew!" Andrew Ledger whistled appreciatively. "Too bad she isn't black."

"Their daughter," Marcia explained. "The private detective insists this is the only footage he could get of her. Not twenty-one yet but she holds fifty thousand shares."

"Who's that?" Brannon asked as a pair of male legs suddenly came into the picture.

"Adam Ward, I think. Apparently our intrepid cameraman couldn't take his mind off the girl."

"Can't blame him," Ledger grinned.

"Not exactly modest, is she?"

Marcia said, "No, not with grandfather. Their relationship is very close, practically incestuous, the townspeople like to say."

"She could make me believe in integration after all," Ledger mumbled. "Maybe black isn't the only color that's beautiful."

"Then she's your assignment," his boss suggested.

"What do you mean?"

"She's yours. Vent your racism on her. It'll make you feel good later, like lancing a boil."

"How's that going to help you get the shares you need?" Marcia asked pragmatically.

As she spoke, the scene before them flicked to the street outside the town's only store. The camera held fast until a man appeared from the inside. He slouched in the old rocking chair on the porch and wiped sweat from his brow with the back of his hand.

Brannon squinted at the face, trying to force his memory back through the years. Was this one of the men, he wondered.

Marcia answered the question for him almost imstantly. "Here's your only chance at control," she said. "Scott Cameron . . . runs the store for the Wards now." At the sound of the name, Brannon clenched his fist and felt cold rage stir deep in his stomach. "He got his hands on twenty-five thousand shares of stock somehow," she added. "Years ago. We don't know the details."

She started to say something more, but on the screen the limp figure of Alfie Ward came from down the street to sit dutifully at Cameron's feet.

"Alfred Ward," Marcia explained. "The half-wit son. You met him."

The film came to an end, and Marica switched on a light.

"And Adam Ward's wife?" Brannon asked. "She used to sing. What about her?"

"You know a lot about this town, boss," Ledger commented.

He paused, waiting for an explanation from Brannon. When none was offered, Marcia went on. "Anyway, she died. Walked in front of a lumber truck about the same time her husband suddenly closed the mill."

Brannon nodded. "And I suppose along about that time, Sid Webster's name stopped appearing on the firm's payroll."

Marcia bent quickly to the file folder on the table. She thumbed through the papers quickly until she found what she wanted. "Sydney H. Webster, logger, suffered a back injury and was put to work running the company spur line. Dropped from the payroll . . . let's see . . . three days before Mrs. Ward committed suicide. Apparently he left town immediately."

Andrew Ledger seemed unimpressed. "A lot of people left town then. The population dropped by thousands. A mill town without a mill."

"Only the rest of them didn't stop using their social security numbers, I'll bet."

"What the hell do we care, boss?" Ledger snapped impatiently. "Dammit, Brannon. There's nothing in Timberland for us. These people have been living on peanuts for years . . . leasing their land, selling old equipment for salvage. They're nobodies. So what are we doing here, playing detectives?"

Brannon reached to the projector and pulled off the reel. He fondled it thoughtfully. "Twenty years ago the Ward family owned a multi-million-dollar operation here. The mill, the rail spur, the timber . . . even the town . . . every house, every place of business. If you worked here, you used company electricity, drank company water, sent your kids to a company school and prayed in a company church. They named the town council and ran the place like a benevolent monarchy. Then in three hellish days, Adam Ward closed the mill and turned his empire into a ghost town. Why? That's the question."

Ledger frowned. "Money. Well, I mean, they must have been going broke."

"No," Marcia corrected. "The firm was no big money-maker, but it was usually in the black."

"And they could have sold the mill for several times what they got by selling the equipment as scrap. They could have gone anywhere, lived like rich people. They didn't have to stay here and watch the town crumble around them."

"They must have a reason."

Brannon said, "Yes. Their past is buried here, and we're going to do the one thing they fear most. We're going to buy this town and dig up that past. Then we're going to smear their noses in it until they choke."

"But why?" Marcia pleaded.

Ledger agreed. "What's in it for us? Where's the profit for Brannon Mills?"

Brannon rose stiffly and laid the reel of film aside. He walked slowly to the patio door and stood with his back toward them.

"Profit?" he said. "Hell, boy, this is why I built Brannon Mills. This is what it's all about."

Andrew Ledger watched his employer go through the sliding glass doors onto the patio, and he felt an urge to go after him.

"Damn him," he said aloud instead. "He treats us like shit, never letting us see the big picture."

Marcia glanced at him cynically and stalked after their boss. At the door she called out to him, her voice plaintive and fragile. "Brannon, wait, please."

She was gone for only a minute, and when she returned, Ledger could see the hurt in her eyes.

"What'd he do? Tell you to get lost?" he taunted.

Marcia kept her back to him as she picked up the beer can near the table and emptied it into the sink behind the bar.

"He called you 'boy,'" she reminded him. "Do you stand for that now?"

Ledger responded defensively. "It's his idea of humor."

"Is it?"

She headed for the stairs and he followed a step behind.

"Well, what about you? He just cut you off, baby. You want him and he turns his back on you like you're overripe fruit."

"Jealous?"

She took several steps up the stairs and his glance fell naturally on her hips.

Rounded. No girdle. Damn her, he thought. He was getting big again.

"Of a rich man," he jeered. "You crazy? Honkies like him could make love every night, but what do they do? They got so tangled up in work, they're through before they're forty."

"Not him," she said from the top of the stairs. "You ever see a woman that didn't turn on when he walked into a room?"

"Nope, but I never saw him take advantage of what he's got either. Now me, that's a talent I'd exploit."

"He's discreet, that's all."

"You sure?" he called as she reached the door to her room. When she had gone from sight, he called once more. "Headed for bed alone? As usual?"

There was no response. He expected none, and for a time he thought he could go back to the bar alone. But in a minute he knew better. He went up the stairs slowly, like a man taking the thirteen steps to the gallows.

At her door he looked in. She stood at the window, and he knew she was watching Brannon on the patio below. She didn't turn when he came up behind her.

"You left the door open," he said, then detested himself for his hypocrisy. He needed no subtle hints from her. He wanted her. He always did when he saw Brannon turn her away. "Still hoping?" he asked cruelly. "Some night, you figure. Some night he'll come in. Don't you ever get tired, just waiting?"

"You shouldn't complain."

He ran his hand along the soft flesh of her arm

and then squeezed hard until she used her other hand to pry his fingers loose. "Why? Because I get to play stand-in? I'm through with that."

"Sure," she said.

Her hands raised to her blouse. She unbuttoned it quickly and went over to the closet to hang it neatly behind her suits.

"I got pride," he said across the bed.

She removed her skirt, hung it beside the blouse and sat on the edge of the bed to take off her hose.

"I don't need you," he told. "It's got something to do with Black Power."

"Try leaving," she grinned, and when she walked past him again she was naked.

She switched out the light and went over to turn down the bed.

When she lay on her back with her legs spread, she told him to take off his pants.

"I know," he grumbled. "And hang them up. You like your room neat."

She laughed lightly from the bed and held out her arms to him when he came to her naked.

He lay on top of her and tried to hate her. He couldn't. There was no depth to his feelings. Although their bodies pressed tightly together, they shared nothing.

It was a bodily function, nothing more, an urge the quiet, powerful man named Brannon had stirred into life. When he plunged ino her, he knew her eyes would be tightly closed. She'd be pretending he was Brannon.

Yet their bodies writhed and slammed at each other with all the violent passion of lovers.

When it was over, though, she cried. She always did and he could feel the moisture of her tears on his cheeks.

He rolled away from her in time to see Brannon standing in the doorway. He saw only the outline of shoulders, of a head, the face blanked in shadows, but he imagined he saw anger in the hidden eyes. Envy turned to rage. He didn't understand, but he felt the hot blade of fear knifing into his belly.

"Brannon?" he said, wanting to reassure himself.

He felt the woman rise up on her elbows. She looked toward the door and said nothing.

Ledger wanted someone to speak, to shatter the agony of silence.

"Say something," he said aloud. "Say anything."

The voice from the door laughed, but there was no mistaking the falseness.

"You there, boy," Brannon joshed. "Don't wear yourself out. You got work to do in the morning."

Then he was gone, and Marcia slithered off the bed. She ran to the door and leaned out into the hallway, screaming.

"Damn you. Goddamn your soul to hell."

"Marcia, don't," Ledger cried. "Don't beg him."

"He wants her," she wept. "That's all he has ever wanted."

"Who?"

"Her, you fool. He'd destroy us all for her."

CHAPTER 8

Catherine paced the living room impatiently, the half-smoked butt of a cigarette dangling from her fingers. "Call him again," she ordered. "They said they'd be here by now."

Obediently, her husband left his chair and picked up the phone, consulting a small pad for the number. The slight hesitation irritated her. She snatched the phone from his hand and dialed. After a dozen rings, she dropped it back on the cradle.

"Easy, Catherine," her father soothed her from the bar. "No need to get impatient."

She sank into a chair and tried to keep her eyes from looking at the others.

They irritated her. All of them. So calm, so boring, this small cluster of people who hovered about her like hungry children at mealtime.

Her husband . . . he never showed his anger, rarely raised his voice, although she knew he seethed and boiled inside from some unknown torment. She had come upon him sometimes in his study, his head down on his arms, his medical books scattered on the floor where he had flung them.

At night he sat before the fire, staring into the flames long after the others had gone to bed. And in winter when the deep snow and the gale winds kept everyone else inside, he wandered into the town alone, disappearing for hours into the deserted buildings.

Her father . . . when she thought of him, she saw a man hunched in a chair, a glass in his hand, and his head nodding in an alcoholic stupor. She had pitied him at first in those months after he watched his wife die beneath the grinding wheels of a truck. She could almost understand why he numbed his mind with liquor while his business empire crumbled around him. And later when she had brought her child home with her from college, there had even been hope. The new life seemed to give him pleasure, and he spent long hours holding the child and whispering softly to her.

Later, with age, he had begun drinking more heavily again until his mind spurted from fogged stupor to bursts of clarity. Eventually she had given up trying to decide whether he was lucid or lost in his own private hell. Like her husband, he stopped talking to her. They passed in the halls and on the stairs without a word until some rare intrusion such as Brannon's invasion shook them all out of their lethargy.

The silence engulfed her daughter too, and as Catherine looked at Louise seated by the window she realized what they had done to the child.

They had stolen all her youth. She had grown through adolescence imprisoned in a home where people rarely spoke, in a town where most of the buildings stood barren and deserted. Walled off from the world by miles of second-growth timber, she lived inside another prison, an unwalled cell that separated her from the few townspeople who remained. Although the town was dead and rotting, she was still Adam Ward's granddaughter, a member of Timberland's faded elite.

And finally, there was Scott Cameron.

In one of his rare ventures beyond the entry hall, he stood nervously near the fireplace. His frayed white shirt was tight at his neck and he fidgeted with his tie as he spoke.

"Right, Mrs. Grossett," he said saying. "No need to fuss. This Brannon guy, he can't hurt us none."

"He only needs one of us," her husband said skeptically.

Catherine glowered at him. "Nobody is selling, I tell you. Nobody."

"Then why is he here?" her father asked. He swirled the ice in his drink and kept his head down. Only when the door chimes sounded, did he look up.

Nobody moved.

The chimes sounded again.

"Somebody better answer it," Louise suggested from her position at the window.

When nobody moved, she left her perch and went out into the hall.

Catherine felt herself holding her breath, waiting for the sound of a voice. When it came, it was not the one she expected.

"I'm Andrew Ledger," she heard the strange voice saying. "Mr. Brannon's assistant."

The black man came into the room ahead of Louise. Immaculately dressed in a conservative business suit, he carried an attaché case.

Nodding politely, he walked directly to the center of the room, placed the case on a table, and opened it briskly.

Only then did Catherine see the second figure standing just inside the entry, seemingly so reticent that the others failed to even notice him.

Brannon, she thought, although she couldn't really see his face.

And Louise—she was standing directly next to the man in the hallway.

Catherine felt an unexpected pang of envy of her daughter, but the voice of Andrew Ledger brought her attention back to the table.

"I believe you are all familiar with my position in Brannon Mills," he was saying, "and if it meets with your approval, I'll get to the point. Now. . . ."

Adam Ward's slurred words interrupted abruptly. "What about Mr. Brannon? Surely he can speak for himself?"

"Mr. Brannon rarely involves himself in negotiations. Now, as I was saying, this is the way it is. Mr. Brannon needs some twenty thousand shares to assume control of Ward Timber Company holdings." Ledger paused to pull a check from beneath a paper clip on one of the file folders. Carefully he placed it openly on the table. "So here is our check for precisely twenty thousand shares. Any one of you is welcome to fill in your name as payee."

Scott Cameron picked up the check. He held it close to his red-lined eyes, but Catherine caught herself seeing only his hands. Thick, pocked fingers. Heavy, dirty nails with the cuticles spreading down to cover the stained white moons. Money would do nothing for him, she thought.

"God!" Cameron exclaimed.

Her husband pressed in closer to glance over the other man's shoulder. He lost none of his composure, but his voice betrayed him as he remarked, "That's two points over the last bid."

Catherine looked past Ledger toward the hallway. "You really do want the company, don't you?" she said.

The others saw Brannon then, and her father took two wobbly steps toward him before he spoke. "Well, you're not getting it. Not at any price."

"That's true," Steve Grossett echoed. "No one will sell."

Deliberately Catherine placed herself between the others and the man in the hall.

"I don't know what you want, Mr. Brannon, but you're not taking over. Not Timberland."

Brannon's reply came back in a whisper. No one was certain he had really heard. It was as though he spoke from a great distance. "A month after I gain control, there will be no Timberland. No stores, no houses, no church, nothing. We'll raze every structure, dig out the foundations."

"But why?" Adam Ward cried.

"That would cost a fortune," his son-in-law whined.

"And what about our stock?" Cameron demanded. "It's all I got."

As a group they stepped toward the hall, but Andrew Ledger crossed in front of them. Behind him the man in the shadows turned and disappeared. They heard the outer door close behind him, before Andrew Ledger began again.

"Obviously Mr. Brannon can't guarantee the value of your stock, even at the current depressed price . . . unless, of course, you're the lucky one who sells him the twenty thousand shares he needs."

Catherine hardly noticed as Ledger returned to the table and replaced his papers in the attaché case. "Well, you know our offer," he said. "I suggest one of you contact me immediately. In private, of course."

"You're bluffing," Adam Ward shouted. "You and your damned Mr. Brannon."

Ledger smiled and headed after his boss. "Mr. Brannon never bluffs," he added as he went out the door.

Behind him Catherine felt a weak numbness gripping her body. She could barely hear as her husband spoke. "He'll do it too. He'll get one of us to sell. Somehow. He'll level Timberland. He'll strip us naked like a hunter dressing out a deer."

"But why?" Catherine asked weakly. "There must be a reason."

"Because he hates you," she heard her daughter say. "Couldn't you sense it in his voice? He's burning with hate."

"But we don't even know him."

"He seems to know us." As she finished the thought, Louise whirled and skipped hurriedly toward the door as though she had suddenly remembered something.

Catherine ran after her, calling, "Where are you going, dear? Not after him."

"Yes," her daughter cried, as she ran along the walk past the privet hedge, toward the two men nearing the car.

Behind Catherine, her grandfather came into the hall.

"Don't go near him, Louise," Adam Ward pleaded. "He's a vile man, a corrupt man."

"He's a man," Catherine said. "That's enough to make you hate him."

Adam Ward stood beside her, propping himself against the door. "Don't make love sound like filth. I just want to protect her."

"From what? You always say that, but you never explain." She faced them both then, her father's sagging shape at the door and her husband coming in from the living room. She flung her words at them, wanting to use them like knives to wound and hurt. "You know, don't you?" she screamed at her husband. "And you," she yelled at Scott Cameron. "You all know, but you never explain. What are we protecting her from? Life?

"Catherine," her husband begged. "We can't quarrel. Not today. And we can't let Louise go to him. She owns stock too."

Her father grasped at her arm, and his fingers felt damp and limp and slimy. "Yes, Catherine, go after her, please."

Catherine thrust his hand away and ran through the porch to the walk. "Louise, wait," she cried as she saw her daughter speak briefly to the tall man at the car.

At the sight of Catherine, Brannon left the girl and stepped into the back seat of the Mercedes.

Louise turned away from the car, her eyes wide with surprise. "Mother, he's so . . ." she stopped, unable to select the word she needed. "I've never seen anyone like him. Powerful, so determined and yet. . . ." She stopped again, apparently noticing the Negro hovering beside her, his face rigid with unexpected concern.

84

"When you're ready to sell, Miss Grossett," he said, "I'm authorized to make the arrangements."

Catherine swept in, took her daughter by the arm, and led her a few paces back up the walk.

"Nobody is selling," she shouted back at Ledger. "Leave us alone."

Louise resisted but her mother hurried her up the walk and back into the house. There the girl burst into tears and ran crying up the stairs. Over Catherine's objections Adam Ward staggered after her.

Alone now, Catherine stood back from the edge of the door and held it open only a crack. She could see the Mercedes still at the curb, the Negro standing beside it, bent over, evidently talking to the man in the back seat.

Brannon was still there, only a hundred feet down the walk, and she felt her entire body warm and uneasy. Her breath came just slightly faster than normal. Her heart thumped in her temples and she felt a need to wet her lips with her tongue.

Why doesn't he leave, she thought. Who is he? What does he really want with us?

And, she wondered, does he know I'm here, watching, waiting like a schoolgirl on her first date?

Almost imperceptibly she opened the door a little wider, hoping he would notice, afraid that he would.

CHAPTER 9

Louise stood brazenly at the window, the curtains pulled back, her face close to the glass. The car was still at the curb, but she could no longer see Brannon.

Yet she knew he was there, in the back seat, his strong, well-manicured hands in his lap, his intriguing face unsmiling. Had he noticed her? She wondered. Really noticed her? And if he had, what had he thought?

At the car they had spoken for just a moment. "Mr. Brannon, I'm sorry," she said.

The family, the town—they had all been inhospitable. She had tried to explain, to apologize for all of them, but the words came hard.

Yet she had gone right up to him. She had never done that before, not with a stranger.

She had felt sorry for him. A man alone in a strange town, just as she was alone.

She tried to tell him all that. But, "I'm sorry," that's all that came out.

He had covered her hand with his, and he smiled. She was certain he understood. Yet she didn't want him to leave. Not yet.

"Louise." She heard her grandfather speak to her

from the door of her room. She didn't want to turn. Not with Brannon's car still parked below.

"Louise," he said again. "Come away from there. He'll see you."

She didn't care. She hoped he would, in fact.

Her grandfather's hand touched her arms, and she thought of a fish coming wet and wiggly from below the surface of the lake.

"That Brannon, he's a horrible man," her grandfather said behind her. "He wants to destroy our town."

"It's already dead," she told him.

He pulled her urgently from the window. His old eyes were red and frightened. "Don't say that," he pleaded. "This is our home. We're happy here."

"Are we?"

"We can't leave Timberland. Not now, not ever."

He mumbled something, but all she could think about was the smell of liquor from his breath.

He clutched at her, bringing their bodies together as he often did.

Today, though, was different. Today he was old and drunk. Not like Brannon at all.

He was crying. She could tell that. He often did when he held her, and she kept her back stiff and erect to support his weight as he sagged against her.

She felt his arm on her breasts. It was his way. He never touched her there with his hand, just allowed his forearm to brush hard across the youthful mounds.

He sobbed again and began sliding down her body. His cheek touched her covered nipple as it never had before.

When his face reached her navel, she pushed him gently away.

He crumpled to the floor and held his head in his hands as though he were going to be sick.

She said nothing.

She left him and went back to the window. Below in the street, the Mercedes was pulling away from the curb.

She felt more alone than ever.

CHAPTER 10

From the back seat of the Mercedes, Brannon saw the figure in front of the store. It took him a moment to recognize the man lolling in the rocking chair.

Alfie's face wasn't obscured, but the white twin mounds he held in front of his shirt were enough to confuse Brannon. The woman's bra was huge, fit for a healthy bovine, and the man in the chair seemed to purr contentedly as he stroked the quilted cotton.

At the sight of the slowly approaching car, Alfie hastily stuffed the bra under his shirt, adding ridiculous twin humps to his own thrust-out chest.

When he recognized the faces in the car, he sprang from the chair and flattened his back against the wall of the store. He whimpered and fled inside.

Brannon could see him hiding himself back of the screen, but he tapped Ledger on the shoulder and gave him instructions to drive past. "Drop me at the house," he told him. "Then stay out of sight for a couple of hours."

Beside him, Marcia shifted the papers on her lap nervously before she spoke. "You think she'll come to you?" she asked.

"Who?"

"Catherine Ward," she told him.

Brannon rested his head on the back of the seat.

He closed his eyes, hoping he'd discourage conversation.

"She'll come," he said eventually.

For a time, they respected his silence, and from the scent of the pines he could tell without opening his eyes that they had left the town and were starting along the narrow road to the lake.

They had gone several miles before Ledger interrupted the soft hum of the engine.

"What about me?" he wanted to know. "What am I supposed to be doing?"

"Get on the daughter," Brannon told him.

"Louise?"

"Yes."

"And do what?"

"Screw her. Or whatever it takes to get her stock."

"You bastards," Marcia said vehemently from his side. "You can't do that. She's just a child."

"Speak for yourself," Ledger told her.

And again the car was quiet. No one spoke until the car made the final turn through the rock-lined garden of the lake house.

At the porch Brannon gave them a few last minute instructions and then he went inside.

In the emptiness of the large living room, he felt unexpectedly alone, and for a time he stood with his back to the closed door, as though he were afraid to go farther. The room with its flowered patterns on the chairs looked so alien to him, no overflowing ashtrays, no papers strewn about. Marcia had seen to that.

He wished he were back at his own apartment near the plant. That was home, although he had never thought of it that way before.

But that's where he should have been, where even the aroma of the rooms was familiar. That's where he should have been waiting for Catherine.

Here in these rented rooms, he was a stranger.

Uncomfortably he tried to make the best of the situation. He moved the furniture about until he had one chair where he wanted it, directly in front of the door, but in the shadows when he pulled the drapes across the window.

Then he fixed a drink, a tall one with lots of ice in case she took longer than he expected. When he had changed his shirt to something more casual, he sat in the chair and waited.

He tried not to think.

There had been too much thinking in all these years. Now it was best just to sit and wait, his eyes fixed on the door.

She would come. He knew she would.

And when he heard another car in the drive, he didn't even shift positions.

"Come in, Mrs. Grossett," he called out when he heard her light feminine knock at the door. "It's open."

She came in hesitantly. She blinked in the dim light and looked about. He didn't rise.

He felt an uneasiness in his chest, a sense of excitement he experienced occasionally when he was closing a deal that would bring in millions.

She was still lovely, he realized again. A work of art in her own way with the brush strokes visible only at the very corners of her eyes.

"Mr. Brannon?" she said as she came farther into the room. When he didn't respond, she came closer still. "You knew I'd come, didn't you?"

He stood then and went to the bar. He fixed a drink and brought it back to her.

"Vodka gimlet," he said. "Your favorite, I believe."

He held the drink so that their hands had to touch as she took it. Their flesh hardly brushed, but her fingers were cool and soft.

"You know why I came," she said.

Deliberately he stepped back from her, just beyond the gentle scent of her perfume. He walked around her, appraising her like a man buying horse flesh. It was a maneuver he had planned for years.

"Yes, I know," he said.

She turned with him, trying to face him, trying to get him into the light where she could see him better. "Then you realize, I'm only interested in. . . ."

Brannon laughed to interrupt her. "You want to save your town," he said, "from me."

"Yes."

Her answer was direct and disarming, but he plunged on, not allowing himself the luxury of thought. He wanted to react according to plan. He had no intention of allowing her to distract him.

"And you told yourself there is only one argument a man like me is susceptible to." He stepped closer again, holding the drink to his lips and looking across the top into her eyes. "You're lovely, Catherine," he said softly.

For a moment she hesitated, apparently shaken by the closeness of their bodies.

"Our lives are here," she spoke out forcefully. "Our memories."

She tried to step away, but he took her arm and pulled her back to him.

"And you'd do anything to protect those memories," he said, "anything to keep them safely behind glass like museum pieces."

"Almost anything. Yes."

He released his grip and let her step away again. When the distance between them was respectably impersonal, he forced his voice to sound like the one he used with his board of directors when he wanted them to know their place.

"All right, Mrs. Grossett," he began. "I'm a reasonable man to negotiate with. You want to keep Timberland. . . ."

"And you want a profit," she added hopefully.

"Profit? Money? I have lots of that. I keep two lawyers busy just telling the government how much I make in a year."

"Then what. . . ."

She stopped as she realized what he was suggesting.

"Don't look away," he told her. "This is strictly business."

She increased the distance between them again, yet she kept her voice low. "You're an attractive man, Mr. Brannon. Surely you don't have to buy your women."

He crossed to her and let the perfume of her body enrage him. He made no attempt to keep the anger from his voice. "I don't buy anything blind, not without seeing what I'm going to get."

Flustered, her voice whined. "What on earth are you implying?" she asked.

"You came here to make a deal," he said. "To trade products. Timberland for a. . . ." He made a motion with his hands, letting her finish the sentence for herself. Then he stepped to the nearest lamp. He tipped back the shade and focused the light on her body. "So take off your clothes, Mrs. Grossett. Let's see what you're offering for this crumbling oasis you call a town."

She stared at him. "You can't be serious."

"But I am. You came here to offer your body. All right, let's have a look at it. Just stand there and take off your clothes. The blouse first, I think."

"I'm no tramp," she cried. "I'm no two-bit slut."

"Of course not, Mrs. Grossett. But isn't it strange; if I had taken you in my arms . . . preferably in the dark . . . if I had coaxed you a little . . . you'd have given yourself. But to stand there in the light . . . just to stand there and strip. . . ."

She flung her glass at him. It struck him in the shoulder and fell to the floor. It didn't even break on the thick carpet, and he kicked it aside as she fled past him toward the door.

When she was gone, he flung open the drapes and stood in the window, watching her car disappear into the trees. Again he felt lonely.

For a long time he sat in the chair, facing the door, hoping she'd come back, but he knew she wouldn't. Not yet. And when sleep came, it came as a welcome relief.

When he awoke, Marcia was bent over him. He couldn't be sure, but he thought she had kissed him on the cheek. "She left angry," she was saying. "You're still pure."

Brannon eased her away and went over to the bar. He poured himself another drink and probed in the empty chest for ice. When he saw Andrew Ledger coming into the house, he thrust out his glass at him. "Get me some ice," he ordered.

Marcia sputtered irritably. "Couldn't you make that a request, not an order, just this once?"

Brannon shrugged. "Orders are best, especially for colored people."

Marcia shrieked. "Brannon, for gawd's sake. . . ."

But Andrew Ledger continued across the room, ignoring the entire exchange. "Cameron's ready to sell," he said excitedly.

Brannon looked surprised. "When?" he asked.

Ledger told him, "Tomorrow. At our offices. He wants cash. No checks."

"What's wrong with here?"

"I don't know. Maybe he's afraid. Anyway he's leaving tonight . . . in his car. I offered to let him fly back with us, but he wasn't interested."

Brannon swished the warm liquor around in his drink and thought about Catherine. He didn't want to leave Timberland just now.

"You can handle it," he told his assistant.

Ledger shook his head. "No. He'll deal with you or nobody. He was quite profane about that point."

Reluctantly Brannon conceded. "Okay. Tell the pilot we'll be going back tonight, right after supper. Now get me some ice."

Ledger looked at him coldly. "Get your own damned ice," he said as he walked toward the stairs. "I've got work to do."

Brannon stood at the foot of the stairs, shouting up at his assistant. "I always said we shouldn't educate you people. Now we have to run our own fool errands."

From the living room, Marcia chided him. "Why

do you treat him like that?" she cried. "He's your friend. Your only friend."

"I know."

"It's not funny to him. He's sensitive. If any other man said anything like that, Andy would kill him. Sometimes I think you hate him. Me too. Everybody."

"Not you or Andy," he said. He came over and kissed her on the cheek like a brother. "Only this town."

He crossed the living room and went out onto the patio. He could hear her come up behind him, but he didn't turn. He kept looking out over the lake where the late-afternoon sun was building its fragile wall of glaring reds and yellows.

From the length of time she stood behind him without speaking, he knew she was going to say something important, important to her at least.

"When this is over," she asked, "when you've destroyed whatever's eating you . . . will it be different with us?"

"Marcia, I'm sorry," he said.

And there was nothing more to say.

He left the patio and walked down toward the lake. He strolled along the shore alone where he belonged.

CHAPTER 11

The dog yapped. He braced his hind feet in the loose gravel, thrust his shoulders forward and barked from deep down in his throat. The big light kept coming. The loud shriek hurt his ears, but he held his ground until the last second.

Then he scrambled off the tracks just ahead of the chugging engine. From the cab, Alfie Ward leaned out and flung a fist-sized chuck of coal. He missed and the mongrel had the last word, a fearless challenge to his fleeing adversary.

Farther down the track at the crossing, the man in the well-dented sedan saw the approaching engine just in time. He slammed on the brakes and skidded to a stop with the dangling bumper only a foot or two from the tracks.

The train stopped too and Alfie grinned out proudly. "Alfie, you damned fool," Scott Cameron cursed from the car window. "You almost killed us."

"That you, Cameron?" Alfie called hopefully, as he came out of the cab.

He approached the car and leaned close to the open window. "Where you goin', Cameron?" he asked.

Cameron pushed him back away from the window

and made a gesture toward the engine. "Get that wheeled teakettle off the road. I'm in a hurry."

Alfie leaned down again, catching a glimpse of another figure on the far side of the front seat. "Who you got in there anyway, Cameron?"

The motor of the car roared, and the tires scraped for a grip on the gravel-sprinkled pavement. The sedan leaped backwards, and then lurched ahead again as Cameron maneuvered for a way around the engine.

"You got that round-assed Alma in there, ain't you?" Alfie yelled as the car dipped into the ditch and headed around the edge of the crossing. "What you want her for?" he screamed at the departing tail lights. "You can't do nothin' with her . . . nothin' you can't do better alone."

Pathetically Alfie Ward trailed the car, his loose limbs flopping and his head bobbing uncontrollably. "Don't go," he yelled into the night. "Please don't go nowhere. Not tonight."

He ran long after the car lights had disappeared toward the highway. He ran across the tracks, past the gaping shell of the depot and through the dark shadows cast by the black frame walls of the deserted auditorium. He didn't stop until he stood in the shaft of light from the store window.

But there was no one inside, he knew. He was alone on the street, and he stood unmoving in his little island of light for a long time. He wasn't afraid, he told himself, not as long as he stood in the light. But he knew it was out there somewhere.

If he stood very still and turned his head slowly, he thought he could hear a rustling sound above the faint restless moan of the breeze. It was there all right, circling probably, waiting in the shadows, poised to leap out at him when he least expected it.

He wasn't afraid, but he hated the way his body lurched and his voice squealed like a woman's when it yapped at him unexpectedly.

Damn dog anyway, he thought. Somebody ought to do something about it.

So he stood in the street for a long time, wishing he had already crossed the unlit distance to the house beyond the privet hedge.

He was still standing there when the lights of a car swept onto the street behind him.

It wasn't Cameron. He was sure of that, but he called his name anyway. Several times he called.

When the lights pointed directly at him like two hands reaching out to choke him, he didn't move. He couldn't. He just stood there and whimpered as the black hulk of a car picked up speed.

With its motor growling fiercely, it rushed toward him out of the night, a black panther closing fast on its prey.

CHAPTER 12

Andrew Ledger yelled. "For Christ's sake, Brannon, watch out."

He lurched across the front seat of the Mercedes, grabbed the ornate steering wheel and jerked it hard to the right. He felt an unexpected resistance in his boss' grip, but the car swerved.

Ahead of them the tall, limp figure of Alfie Ward loomed as the left front fender brushed his arm and the headlights flared brightly in his frightened eyes for a fraction of a second.

The car skidded to a stop.

In the back seat Marcia gasped.

Mechanically Brannon's hand worked the gear shift, and the car pounced back from the curb. This time Ledger was too stunned to react. Helplessly he gaped through the rear window as the flame red of the tail lights blazed in Alfie's startled face.

Marcia's scream drowned out the sound of the brakes, but the abrupt stop snapped Ledger's head back against the seat like the end of a whip.

The car was already rolling down the street again before the big black man was certain that Alfie still stood upright in the light from the store.

He squinted across the seat and tried to read his

boss' expression. In the darkness he saw only rigid, stiff lines that he didn't understand.

Incredulously Ledger flung the accusation at him. "You tried to hit him. Not once, but twice."

"Did I?" Brannon answered stiffly.

Ledger tried to organize the mixed thoughts that flicked through his mind. "Back at the lake," he said. "You wanted to drive. You. . . ."

He stopped and peered through the rear window. Alfie hadn't moved.

Then Marcia said it for him. "You wanted to scare him," she cried at Brannon. "That poor, sick man. You almost frightened him to death. Why? Why him?"

Angry now, Ledger thrust his foot across the floor console and jammed his instep onto the brake. The car bucked to a stop and Brannon straightened in the seat, his hands still fixed on the steering wheel.

"All right, Brannon, I've had it," he snapped. "You and your damned secrets."

"Andy, please," Marcia soothed.

"No," Ledger growled. "No more stalls. This time I want facts. What the hell are we doing in this wooden graveyard? What are we trying to buy? Why did you come within an eyelash of killing that halfwit? We got a right to know. This isn't just business anymore. You're involving us. You're. . . ."

He stopped, realizing Brannon had ceased to listen. As if he had heard nothing from his assistant, he stared through the windshield toward the old millpond.

In a trance, without moving the direction of his gaze, Brannon opened the door and slipped out.

Leaving the door hanging open, he walked away into the darkness.

"Well, I'll be damned," Andrew Ledger exclaimed as he watched his boss disappear toward the pond.

As Brannon passed the privet hedge and crossed the open space between the Ward house and the pond, the wind grew stronger until he had to lean his big frame against it. Occasionally it dried his eyes and made it difficult to see, but he kept the single point of light in sight.

Within twenty yards of the gnarled tree, he called out expectantly.

"Catherine?"

When there was no answer, he moved closer until he could easily make out the figure in the full, white dress. He called again and held out his hand, thinking she had reached out to him too.

"Not Catherine," the figure whispered. "Louise."

And as he came closer, he realized his error and momentarily felt the sinking sensation of disappointment.

The girl was lovely, of course. She held a cigarette awkwardly to her lips, and its glow illuminated the smoothly perfect features of her face, yet he wished it was Catherine instead.

"You called my mother's name," the girl said. "Has it been you . . . all these years?"

"What?"

"The light by the tree. Was it you? Before I mean?"

"You've seen lights at night? Here?" he asked.

"Yes. By the tree, this ugly, lovely tree. As long as

I can remember. Sometimes I thought I saw a face in the glow of a cigarette. Sometimes I thought. . . ."

"It wasn't me."

"I used to think it was mother, meeting a lover. But there's no one, not in Timberland, no one she would want."

"You can never be sure."

"I know my mother. It would have to be someone special. Like you."

"Thank you."

Louise laid her hand on the trunk of the twisted tree and ran her fingers along the bark, caressing it, he thought, as one might fondle a memento from a night of love.

She seemed far away suddenly, as though they didn't really share the same small plot of ground, set apart by the night from the rest of the world.

Catherine's child, he thought. From her body, from her flesh. He felt a warmth he hadn't known very often before. A bit of Catherine stood with him.

And Grossett too.

Brannon felt angry again. The girl was Grossett's child too. His seed inside of Catherine, growing, maturing, becoming this, a child, a woman.

He should hate the girl, he knew. But he wouldn't. Instead he'd use her.

"Am I too young for you?" the girl asked abruptly.

He smiled faintly. "I'm twice your age."

She came closer. "No man has ever kissed me," she said. "Just boys with girlish voices at school. Now, even they're afraid."

"Of whom?"

"Grandfather. If a boy so much as looks at me, he chases the whole family out of town. He'd die if someone touched me. Mother too. She's just as bad."

They were so close now, she had to look up to see into his eyes and he could sense the aroma of her perfume, the same her mother had worn earlier.

"And now a man like you comes," she said, "a torrent after the drought. We're so parched, mother and I, a look and you'd drown us."

"I'm here on business," he told her flatly.

"No, you're not. You came to hurt someone. Mother, I think." With transparent coyness, she raised her hand and touched his shoulder. "If you hate her so much, you could take me." Their bodies touched lightly, and he smiled at her amateurish advances. "You could pretend to love me," she suggested. "That would torment her . . . him too."

"That would take time."

"Not if I help."

"You know what you're saying."

"Yes, I've read books. I'm stealing the words from one now."

"Why?"

"Because when you're gone, there'll be no one. There'll be nothing."

He pulled her to his chest and felt the twin pressures of her breasts. He remembered that from before, the way it had been, what a touch had done to his body.

Urgently he pulled her tighter until he was crushing her to him. They touched at the navel and she thrust in her hips tentatively.

"Pretend, Mr. Brannon. Pretend we're lovers like in the books. And there's only tonight."

He kissed her gently.

When their lips parted again, she smiled up at him.

"Hate them more," she said, and she pressed in hard, making slow, circular motions with her lower belly. "Imagine they're watching. Imagine they're seeing me pressed against you, knowing how I'm feeling deep inside."

She placed her hand behind his head and kissed him with an open mouth. Her tongue forced its way past his lips and sought out his. When he didn't respond, she stopped long enough to whisper in his ear. "And they are watching. Both of them."

He looked past her shoulder toward the house and saw the upper window. He wasn't sure but he thought he saw a motion there, a movement of a curtain, a vague suggestion of a light.

Tortured with his own fury, he placed his hand squarely on the girl's buttocks and forced her in against the fly of his trousers.

"Damn!" he cursed. "Damn you all."

Misled by the source of his passion, the girl laughed insanely and coaxed him toward the ground. "Punish them, Brannon," she screamed. "Punish them for what they've done to me."

They sank together beneath the gnarled tree, and he spread her out on the ground like a table cloth. Then, with a finesse recalled from far back in his memory, he kissed her passionately while his hands found the top button of her dress.

She squirmed and writhed beside him as she shrugged the dress off her shoulders. When her small but youthful breasts were opened to him, he touched his lips against the cool, smooth flesh, then moved downward until the hotter coarser flesh of the nipples grew tight and erect.

Even as his hands moved down her body, he looked to the house and tried to listen for the sound of someone approaching. But there was nothing. He and the girl seemed alone in an empty world.

And the only groans were hers.

Then suddenly appalled, he thrust her aisde and stood above her.

"Brannon, don't," she cried. "Don't go."

He straightened his clothes and backed away from the tree. "I'll be back," he said. "Later."

"No," she pleaded. "Later, I'll be afraid. Brannon!"

But he was gone, walking briskly toward the car that still sat at the front of the house.

She stood, her fingers fumbling with the front of her dress.

"Please," he heard her cry.

But as he reached the car, his attention was on the house. He wanted the door to open, for one of them to come out, to see, to know he had been with their child in the weeds by the pond.

And he knew they were watching even before the front door flew open.

He felt pleasure as he recognized the hunched figure of Adam Ward silhouetted on the porch. He saw Catherine too and he knew they had seen what he was doing to Louise.

Even Ledger and Marcia had guessed. He could tell by their expressions when the dome light of the car caught the blend of fascination and horror in their faces.

They said nothing as he slipped into the seat and started the engine.

He meant to pull away immediately, to avoid the figures running toward him from the house, but he wasn't fast enough. From the other direction, Louise was coming through the opening in the hedge. The car lights glared at her.

Her white dress hung from one shoulder, her hair was a tangled ball of yarn, and her face was gnarled with an inner agony.

"B-r-a-n-n-o-n," she cried in a long, mournful wail.

But the car swept past her, leaving her on the walk, her arms held out to him plaintively.

They were nearly to the airport at Chestertown before Ledger broke the silence.

"What'd you do to her, Brannon? Why was she screaming?"

Brannon looked directly at him. There was no remorse in his answer. "I was doing your job for you."

"What are you talking about?"

Marcia whimpered from the back seat. "You did that? But she's just a child."

"What in God's name are you, Brannon?" Ledger demanded. "An animal?"

Brannon shook his head. "Not quite. Not a man. Not quite an animal either."

CHAPTER 13

Her face wracked with pain, her cheeks streaked with tears, Louise stood at the curb watching the car disappear into the black tunnel of trees that led out of town.

Her grandfather reached her first. His shaking hands clasped at her dress and tried to lift the cloth back into place. He wept and screamed unintelligible and vile epitaphs in the direction of the road.

Her mother reached her next. With an arm she pulled her daughter protectively to her breast.

Then came Grossett. Less hurriedly, he came out of the house and walked to the curb. "What is it?" he asked. "What happened?"

"It's Brannon," Adam Ward shouted. "I think he raped her."

"No," Grossett said firmly.

Ward looked toward his son-in-law, but Louise stiffened erect and spoke for herself.

"He wouldn't have me," she said. "I threw myself at him, but he walked away."

"Louise, don't," her mother cautioned.

Adam Ward placed his wrinkled hands on the girl's cheeks and brought her face to his. He kissed her comfortingly, then clutched her to his body. "My baby," he drooled.

113

Steve Grossett's mouth twisted with disgust. "Adam, stop it," he groaned.

From the direction of the store, came a scream. It started low in a human throat and grew to an animal's howl.

Together, the people by the house whirled and faced toward the shaft of light from the store.

Screaming from the tormented depths of his fogged mind, Alfie stood in the center of the main street, the black, deserted buildings seeming to tower above him.

He was naked. His clothes lay scattered about him.

In his hand he held a stout strip of rope. Blood stained the thick cord here and there along its length.

Welts striped his body, creating a crisscross along his shoulders and down across his legs. Yet his huge penis hung stiff and full from his body.

The people from the house ran toward him, all except Louise. Gagging on the horror of what little she could see from a distance, she broke and ran into the house.

Her grandfather, though, stumbled drunkenly to his son. "Alfie, no, not again," he cried.

As if on signal, lights came on in the scattered houses still occupied far down the empty street. A few residents came running in nightclothes. Twenty yards from the store, they stopped, then approached more cautiously.

The oldest, a feeble man in his eighties, came close until he could see. Then he lost interest. He had seen Alfie punish himself before.

Frantically Adam Ward gathered clothing from

the street and thrust the trousers toward his son. But Alfie, with his mouth hanging open, made no move to cover himself.

"Go home," his father yelled at the dark figures in the street. "You've seen him before. There is nothing new here."

When no one backed away, Ward stiffened his shoulders and stepped threateningly toward the small knot of townspeople.

"Go ahead then," he cried. "Gape at us. The Wards . . . the almighty Wards . . . naked in the street. But in the morning you'll move. All of you. Out of Timberland. You hear?"

With the threat, the group broke and walked slowly to their homes. The feeble old man was the last to leave and he spit once in the gutter before he was gone.

At the store Catherine had gotten one of her brother's legs into his trousers and was trying to get him to lift the other.

"We'd better get Cameron," her husband suggested. "He can usually bring Alfie out of it."

Catherine shook her head. "Cameron's gone."

Ward and her husband looked at her, apparently puzzled.

"His wife called," she said. "In hysterics. Cameron ran off with that Alma."

"But how could he?" Grossett asked sharply. "Cameron never has any money. He never. . . ."

He raised his eyes and looked down the street and along the road that the Mercedes had taken a few moments before."

"Brannon!" Adam Ward whispered.

His son-in-law nodded. "Yes. Brannon."
"We'll have to stop them."
"Of course."

CHAPTER 14

In the passenger compartment of the jet, Brannon came awake slowly. He felt a little stiff around his neck and the day's growth of beard on his chin made him feel soiled, but the rest had been welcomed.

"We let you sleep," Marcia said from the aisle.

He pushed back the small drapes at the oval window and let the sun stream in.

"It's morning," she added. "We got back last night. I hated to wake you."

She held out his electric razor and toothbrush. "I got some things from your apartment. There's a fresh outfit in the head."

He patted her affectionately on the cheek and went into the cramped toilet at the rear of the plane. His clean suit and shirt hung against the back of the door. Fresh underwear was stacked next to the stainless steel sink.

"Coffee's ready too," she called to him from outside.

When he came out of the toilet and took the coffee, he kissed her on the cheek.

"Why the hell aren't you married?" he asked. "You'd make a good wife."

"You never asked," she told him.

He watched her well-shaped hips as she moved up

the aisle ahead of him, and for a moment he wanted to tell her, to explain. But he wouldn't, he knew. If he did, he'd be even more alone.

"That man named Cameron," she was saying officiously. He's here. Must have driven all night. He wants to see you immediately."

He opened the cabin door for her and they went out onto the small ramp.

Coming toward them, from the rear entrance to the plant, was Ledger.

There was no smile on his face. "You finally up, boss? Well, we got troubles. Big troubles."

"Cameron?" Brannon asked.

Andy Ledger appeared disgruntled. "No. The Ward clan. The old man. Catherine. The son-in-law. They're all in your office. Drove in first thing this morning."

Brannon raised his eyes toward the penthouse office atop the administration building. He wondered if they were looking down upon him from above.

"Did they get to Cameron?" he asked. "Did they make him change his mind?"

Ledger said, "No. They don't know he's here for sure. He's out in the mill, scared to death the Wards will talk him out of selling."

"And that woman he's with? Where is she?"

"The one named Alma?"

"Yes. I guess that's her name."

"Waiting for him in the car," Marcia interrupted. "I had him park back in the employees' lot."

"All right. Stall the others until I can see Cameron and close the deal. Have you got the check?" he asked Ledger.

Ledger pulled a check from an inside pocket and

passed it across. "Only there's another problem," he said. "Cameron wants cash."

"Let me worry about that," Brannon took the check and walked swiftly across the runway to the plant entrance.

He was whistling cheerfully as he passed the towering stacks of paper scrap and followed the shining tracks of the rail spur. Around him cranes hoisted tons of paper like giant, white tootsie rolls, while rumbling, overhead, conveyor belts spewed a steady stream of wood chips onto the pinnacles of already mountainous cones.

Workers spoke to him diffidently, their voices drowned in the rumble of the massive equipment, but he ignored them as he passed, his eyes fixed on the corrugated metal of the mill and his thoughts on the man who waited for him inside.

Inside he spoke briefly to a single man in a hard hat, and followed his pointing arm along the metal catwalk that ran past the roaring chipper toward the debarking chamber.

He climbed along the labyrinth of railed catwalks and found Cameron huddled against the grating that shielded a whirring circular saw. Behind him the blade peeled a slice from a mammouth trunk as he tried to shout something at Brannon.

Unable to hear above the buzzing roar, Brannon took the quaking man by the arm and led him through the heavy door of the debarking chamber control room. On the other side of the protective glass, the powerful jets of water stripped a log bare and another rumbled down into position. But Brannon tapped the operator on the shoulder and made a motion toward the door with his thumb.

The man nodded, left his control panel, and stepped outside.

Even without the hydraulic blast of the debarker, the cramped room rattled and shook from the surrounding equipment, and Cameron had to shout to make himself understood.

"You got the money?" he yelled.

Brannon held out the check.

"Yeah," he called. "Just cash it. The endorsement is the only contract we need."

Cameron's weathered face twitched with excitement, but he pushed the hand away. "No. No checks. Cash. I ain't goin' to no bank." When he saw the hesitancy in Brannon's face, he produced a folded stock certificate and handed it to him. "Bring a pen. I'll sign as soon as I get the dough."

Brannon unfolded the intricately etched certificate and felt his hands quaver.

Finally, he thought, after so many years, a scrap of paper and it was his . . . Ward's company, the town, practically everyone in it too. They'd be his to destroy as deliberately, as slowly as he wanted.

"All right," he said. "It'll take me a few minutes. Want to wait somewhere more comfortable?"

"No. You get it. Bring it here."

He leaned back against the glass partition, his face growing smug and contented. Suddenly he was no longer afraid.

As Brannon turned to leave, he called out to him. "What do you want it for, Brannon?" he asked. "A ghost town . . . nothing there but unpainted shacks. A guy like you, you already got everything. What can you get out of Timberland?"

Brannon found the word carefully.

"Truth," he answered.

"What?"

"Like what happened twenty years ago? What made old man Ward suddenly close down the mill? Why did his wife walk in front of a log truck?"

The fear raged again in Cameron's face. The answer had come back so unexpectedly. He felt befuddled, like a child being grilled by a cruel parent.

"Twenty years ago? What the hell do you care?"

He felt his body grow cold and yet there was sweat oozing out in the wrinkles around his powerful neck. He wanted to run. He wanted to grab back the certificate and escape through the door, but Brannon blocked the way.

"Maybe I knew Webster," Brannon was saying, his voice distant, buried somewhere in the clanking and rumbling of the plant noises. "Maybe we were friends."

"Sid Webster?" Cameron whispered the name, a name he hadn't uttered aloud in years.

"You remember him. Used to sit in front of the bar . . . drinking beer . . . making bets."

Cameron's stomach knotted and squeezed in on itself. He wanted to retch. The fear that began deep in his intestines was written all over his face. "What kinda bets?" he yelled suspiciously.

"Weird bets," Brannon told him. "With soldiers. You remember. About girls."

Cameron's mouth sucked hard for a breath. His mind was telling him things he couldn't bring himself to believe. "How'd you know about Webster? How'd you know about. . . ."

Suddenly he pushed himself away from the glass partition and reached out for Brannon. He put his hand on the other man's face and tipped his chin to let the light fall across the scarred cheek. He had seen that cheek before, at night in the forest with blood spreading from the cut that was now a scar.

"You!" he said. "The soldier."

Instinctively he pulled back his arm and lashed outward, whipping Brannon across the face. "You crud. You came back," he screamed.

Brannon staggered against the wall and slumped to his knees. Cameron kicked him hard in the stomach. "You got no right to come back." He charged in, raising his fists like hammers, but the man on the floor rolled aside and came up fighting.

From behind, he caught Cameron around the neck and tightened his grip. "I got no right?" he cried. "After what you did to me?"

Cameron dug his nails into the arm at his neck and gained a fraction of an inch, enough to gurgle in a breath. "Us?" he choked. "A few bruises, a few scratches. That's all you paid for the only beautiful thing in town."

"All? A few bruises?" Brannon laughed sadistically and tried to retighten his grip.

"Go ahead," Cameron challenged. "Kill me. Maybe they'll shove you in a cell for another murder."

He let his hands fall limp at his side, and for a second Brannon squeezed out his breath. Then slowly his grip relaxed.

He shoved Cameron away, knocking him to the floor. He made no effort to rise immediately.

"The town," Cameron said. "You killed it. You left us sterile and dying."

"You were there that night too."

Painfully Cameron got to his feet. His hand checked his neck and he had difficulty getting out the words. "I've hated myself ever since. Watching Catherine all these years . . . that beautiful body wasted. And Adam Ward, a powerful man gone dry, hating the very thing he loves most."

"That doesn't excuse what you did to me."

Carefully Brannon watched the man's face, looking for a sign, a reaction that would tell him what he wanted to know. Was it Cameron? Was he the one that had come back that night with the knife?

"We hardly touched you," Cameron recalled. "We should have killed you."

Cameron made a step toward the door, but Brannon flung him back against the glass.

"One of you came back that night. Was it you, Cameron? Tell me, dammit."

"I don't know what you're talking about." Cameron tried again for the door, but Brannon blocked the way with his body. "And get out of my way. I ain't selling you nothin'. Not any more."

Brannon grinned. "You'll sell. Or I'll get the stock I need from the girl."

"Louise?" Cameron gasped. "You son of a bitch, you would. Just like you did her mother."

"Why not?"

"Because. . . ." Cameron stopped himself, reconsidering. Then his shoulders sagged in defeat. "All right. I'll sell, but you leave them alone. Both of them . . . Louise and Catherine . . . or I'll come back and cut your heart out."

Brannon smirked. "No, you won't, Cameron. Once I start bulldozing those old buildings, you won't be around."

"You are a bastard."

Brannon opened the door, then hesitated. He studied the other man one more time, making up his mind as he did. "It really wasn't you, was it?"

"What's that mean?" Cameron asked.

"That night. You didn't come back. With the knife. She didn't mean that much to you, did she?"

"I don't know what the hell you're talking about. Just get the money. Me and Alma. We want to be in Mexico by tonight. We're gonna fly from Frisco. We never been on a plane. Neither of us."

"Sure, Cameron, sure. Tonight . . . you and that Alma . . . real heaven."

He slammed the door behind him. Outside on the ramp, the operator came back toward him, but Brannon took his pack of cigarettes from his pocket and tossed it to him.

"Take a break," he told him. "Tell your lead man Brannon said it was okay."

The worker touched his hardhat in a mock salute and started up the catwalk toward the open bay above. Behind him Brannon headed down and out of the mill.

He was whistling in spite of the cut on his lip.

In Brannon's office, Steve Grossett stood at the window, looking down at the jet parked near the plant entrance. He had seen Brannon leave the aircraft and watched him go into the woodmill. He saw him come out again now and followed him as he left the plant and crossed the street to the town's only bank.

Behind him Catherine mumbled irritably to herself. "This is ridiculous . . . driving all night. We don't even know Cameron came here."

She sat in the leather swivel chair at the big mahogany desk and soiled the amber glass ashtray with another filter-tipped cigarette butt, the fifth since they had arrived.

On the far side of the desk, Adam Ward nosed about the room, pulling books thoughtfully from the shelves and tentatively opening cabinets. When he found the liquor, he closed the cabinet sharply and turned his back on it.

"He'll never sell his stock," Ward said finally. "He knows I'd kill him if he did."

At the hall door, the pretty black secretary came in carrying a tray filled with cups and saucers. "Coffee, folks," she beamed happily. "Or I'll bring tea if you prefer. I'm sure Mr. Brannon will be up in a minute. He's usually quite prompt."

Grossett took one final look out the window and came around the desk. Smiling with mock sheepishness, he made his way toward the hall door. "Excuse me a minute," he said. "It was a long ride."

The young secretary appeared surprised. "Oh, there's a washroom here, Mr. Grossett."

But it was too late. Already Grossett was in the hall and disappearing toward the stairs.

At the desk, Catherine glanced sharply toward her father as she sensed something unusual in her husband's abrupt disappearance.

"What is it?" she asked her father.

The old man frowned. "I don't know." Then, thinking of something important, he put aside the book he held. "Wait here," he suggested.

Trying to appear casual, he stepped briskly to the

door. "I think I'll have a look around the plant while we're waiting," he said.

The secretary almost dropped the tray. "Oh, Mr. Ward, I don't know if you should," she began hesitantly. "I mean. . . ."

"Oh, Miss," Catherine interrupted deliberately. "Do you have saccharin? I hate to be a bother, but you know how it is, dieting and all."

In the hall Adam Ward called to his son-in-law. "Steve, wait. What's wrong?"

He caught up with him at the staircase and they went down together.

"I have a hunch Cameron's here," Grossett told him when they reached the plant level.

Ward's voice wavered. "Meeting Brannon? But he can't sell. He's as much involved as we are." He tried to hold his son-in-law back but the younger man shook free. "You've got to stop them, Steve. If Brannon gets control, he'll dig and probe . . . like Alfie . . . nosing around, opening our pasts like a tomb."

"Don't tell me what I have to do, you old fool. It's more your problem than mine."

"But what'll we do? We can't let Cameron sell."

"Get to Cameron first," Grossett shouted as they entered the plant. "Do what you should have done years ago."

Leaving Ward behind, Grossett crossed the main floor of the plant. The older man watched him go, then slowly headed toward the nearest exit.

In the control room of the debarking chamber, Scott Cameron lit another cigarette. He knew better.

He didn't need the sign on the wall to warn him, but he needed the smoke to steady his hands.

The glow was almost down to the filter when the metal door clanged open ahead of him.

"Brannon, that you?" he asked, before the door was fully opened.

When he recognized his error, he started to smile. Then his face went white with shock.

"You!" he gasped. "How'd you know."

The outstretched hands plunged for his throat, the thumbs together, the fingers forming a vise.

"Hey, don't," he screamed, but the hands were at his neck, pressing hard. "For Christ's sake, I didn't tell him anything."

Flinging his arms upward, he broke loose, but the dark figure in front of him picked up something heavy and lunged at him again. The metal object glanced off Cameron's ear and knocked him to his knees. Blood squirted from his temple.

Another blow missed him by inches and he scrambled across the steel floor. Through his blurred vision he saw the unlocked opening to the inner chamber. He went that way in desperation, stumbling and tripping as he tried to make his way across the slick, wet flooring to where the logs rolled into the debarker.

Even before he heard the roar of the water jets, he saw the face on the far side of the protective glass. He heard the next log tumbling toward him.

He screamed and screamed again, his feet and hands scratching at the metal walls, but there were only seconds before the powerful jets knocked him beneath the rolling log.

In the warm sun of the late afternoon, Adam

Ward, his daughter, and his son-in-law sat together, their cocktail glasses empty and dry. Behind the mahogany desk, Brannon folded his hands patiently, but the lines around his eyes showed his weariness.

"All right, Mr. Brannon," the Sheriff was saying from his place near the door, "if you say so, but it'll be up to the coroner's jury to decide if it's suicide or not." The long, thin man with the bald head sighed and replaced his cap. "I can't figure anybody picking that way to die." He closed his small notebook and tucked it away in his shirt pocket.

From the way he moved, Brannon knew the man in the uniform wasn't satisfied, but almost an entire day of investigation had turned up nothing. Cameron had been dead when they found his battered body buried in the soaking black chips of the debarking chamber.

No one had been seen entering. No one had been seen leaving. The suicide suggestion came as close to a solution as anything proposed so far.

"What about us?" Steve Grossett asked. "Can we start back? We have a long drive."

The Sheriff produced his political smile and nodded pleasantly. "Certainly, folks. I appreciate your identifying the body. Kinda ugly business."

"About the body," Grossett continued. "We'll want to bury it in Timberland. I've called the widow and. . . ."

"Sure, anytime. No question about the cause of death." The thin man tipped his hat and opened the hall door. "See you later, Mr. Brannon."

"Right, Sheriff," Brannon nodded.

When he had gone, Brannon went to the open

bottle on the counter and poured himself another drink. "My pilot will take you back," he said to Catherine. "Save you hours of driving."

"We don't want anything from you, Brannon," her husband told him coolly.

"Just leave us alone," Adam Ward said as he followed his son-in-law into the hall.

The last to leave, Catherine paused, looking back at Brannon. "That man is dead because of you," she said. There was no anger in her voice, only the flatness of her voice accused him.

Behind her Andrew Ledger and Marcia came into the room. She seemed to ignore them as she made one final plea. "If you hadn't wanted his stock, he'd still be alive. Perhaps now you'll leave us alone."

Brannon waited until she was gone, then he spoke softly as though she were still there to hear. "He's been a long time dying," he said.

Ledger frowned. "Who? Cameron?"

Brannon turned his back on them as he stood at the window, looking down at the street.

"Yes," he said.

Marcia's voice sounded puzzled. "You wanted Cameron dead?"

"Maybe it wasn't an accident," Ledger accused.

Brannon seemed unimpressed. "It's not important. He wasn't the one I'm after."

"Then who? Who the hell are you trying to destroy?"

"I don't know. Not yet. But he's been expecting me for twenty years, knowing I'd be back, knowing sooner or later I'd figure out which one he is. And maybe it's time I re-introduced myself. Maybe I ought to tell them. The soldier is back and he's going to strip the cover off that town like you'd peel an artichoke."

"You're crazy."

Brannon opened the attaché case on his desk and tossed in the unsigned stock certificate from his jacket pocket.

"Of course," he said. "Crazy with hate. Somebody in that town cut me off from the world . . . left me to wander alone through a cauldron of flesh." He closed the case with a snap. "Brains, money, power . . . I have it all. An empire, but I'm alone on the street, peeking into the whorehouse window."

Marcia stepped in front of him. "Brannon, you're sick," she said.

"So's the world. It's one big madhouse and all the doctors have gone home for the night."

"Wait," Ledger pleaded. "Where are you going?"

Brannon laughed as he answered. "To a funeral. A bon voyage party, I guess you'd call it."

CHAPTER 15

Overhead the dark clouds rolled and boiled, a black, misty surf seeking a distant shore. Around the perimeter of the town, the trees strained against the erratic wind, their outer limbs flapping nervously in anticipation of the threatening storm.

In the town Alfie Ward sounded his engine's whistle importantly. He had been building steam for hours in preparation. He could see the front car of the procession moving slowly along the street from the church, but he could not resist the urge to hurry them on with a loud and impatient blast.

Still fretting over his key part in the occasion, Alfie swung down out of the cab and ran back along the track. He checked the couplings between the coal and flat cars again and then made a final inspection of the linkage to the caboose.

It was the longest train he had pulled in years. The last time had been a funeral too, and the other men in town, they'd had to help him remember how the equipment worked.

They would let him drive, though. All the way up the grade to the cemetery. They had to. It was his engine.

Wind, cold and mournful for summer, whipped the dust in the street ahead of the lead car, but it reached the tracks without hesitation and slowed gently to a stop. Behind that came the pickup truck.

Alfie could see the casket protruding from the tailgate. Cameron was in there, but he didn't like to think about that. Alfie didn't understand being dead.

The other cars, nearly a dozen in all, stopped in order. None of the doors opened for a time, and Alfie shifted nervously on his feet. The machines seemed animate, and he felt as though he were alone in the world, with a mechanical snake poised before him on the street.

Eventually Scott Cameron's older brother got out of the lead car. Adam Ward came out next, graciously holding the arm of the widow. A fat woman, she wore a black housedress that drooped at the hemline and seemed about to fall free from her shoulders. She kept her head down as she waddled alongside Ward to the steps at the rear of the caboose.

It took three men to help her aboard.

Grossett, with his wife and daughter, emerged from the first car back of the truck. He took the women to the caboose and then stayed outside to silently direct the procession.

When most of the women were inside, men appeared from the cars and hoisted the heavy casket from the truck. They carried it gingerly to the flat car and placed it in the center. Others handed up flowers to be laid beside it.

Alfie watched with open mouth, his eyes fixed on the casket until a sharp, yapping sound from behind the cars caught his attention.

The belligerent mongrel charged at the engine, his

teeth bared and ready, but one of the townsmen swept it up in his arms and carried it toward the flat car.

Alfie sputtered in protest until a car approaching from the direction of the highway made him forget the fierce little animal momentarily. He recognized the Mercedes and felt a new sense of fear.

The car rolled to a stop and Brannon stepped out.

From the back of the caboose, Adam Ward cursed. "Damn! What's he doing here?"

Louise appeared from inside. She smiled hopefully and squeezed past her grandfather.

"Mr. Brannon," she called.

Her father tried to stop her as she ran to the Mercedes, but there was no slowing her until she stood within inches of Brannon. Although he looked past her to the train, she squealed up at him expectantly. "You came back. Is this the later you promised."

He pulled her close as though to kiss her. "The whole town is watching," he said.

"I know."

He kissed her lightly on the cheek before her grandfather shouted at her with jealous impatience. "Louise, you're holding up the procession."

She kissed Brannon as ardently as he would permit and tugged on his sleeve. "Come with us," she begged.

The engine whistle blasted and the mongrel dog barked his protest at this new offense to his ears. The rest of the townsmen swung aboard.

"Please," Louise asked. "Pretend we're lovers. It's like going to church together."

Brannon glanced toward the sky, measuring the time before the clouds unleashed themselves on the forested mountain below.

"All right," he conceded.

He returned to the car and spoke to Andrew Ledger who sat in the driver's seat.

"Wait," he ordered.

Ledger nodded but his secretary leaned forward from the back. "Don't you want us with you?" she asked. "You might not be safe alone."

He smiled noncommittally and went with Louise to the rear of the train. He started to mount the metal stairs, but Adam Ward poised above him. "You got no business here," the old man challenged. "We're burying one of our own."

"A man you murdered," Brannon said as he passed. "You or that son-in law of yours."

Adam Ward's bloodshot eyes widened at the accusation, but he said nothing.

The train lurched ahead. The whistle blew again. The dog yapped. Flowers fell away from the casket and littered the edge of the track. On the flat car the men sat stiffly reverent and thrust their faces doggedly into the growing wind.

Brannon deliberately paused in the doorway to the swaying, rattling caboose. He wanted the women inside to see him clearly. They met him first with contempt in their tired eyes. Women in cheap dresses long used only for church and funerals, they saw him as the threat they had been told to expect. When he smiled, though, their eyes softened, and he could imagine the youth they had enjoyed once, ever so briefly.

The woman he sought, the widow, sat at the far end of the car. With her was Catherine Ward, but he ignored her for the fat one.

He squeezed in beside her and she looked up curiously through her profusely flowing tears.

"Leave her alone," Catherine Ward said across her, and for a moment Brannon thought she had guessed his purpose. "Leave my daughter alone," Catherine added. "There is nothing in Timberland for you now, with Scott gone."

Brannon ignored her and reached into his breast pocket. He brought out his checkbook and pen. He unfolded the checks on his knees and began to scribble.

He didn't have to look up to sense the reaction around him. Adam Ward and his son-in-law leaned forward from their benches. A woman at the far end stood. The widow wiped a moist handkerchief across her eyes. And Louise Ward giggled.

"Brannon, not here," her mother whispered. "Not now."

Steve Grossett took a threatening step forward. "You're disgusting Brannon."

"Have you no decency, man?" Adam Ward asked. "This is a funeral, not a boardroom."

But the window's sobs ceased as she saw him add her name to the check. He held it out to her, and for a second, he thought he saw her hand start toward it. Instead she raised her eyes and looked about the crowded car.

She lowered her head and raised the handkerchief back to her eyes, but the sobbing was softer now.

He was winning, he knew.

With the checkbook back in his pocket, he closed

his eyes and shut out the belligerence he felt around him. He used the technique often in business meetings. In his private darkness he was impregnable.

But today he could still smell Catherine's perfume. He still knew Louise was watching him. Even the darkness didn't help.

When the engine slowed, Brannon opened his eyes again. The car had grown darker, colder, the people inside more withdrawn from each other as they suffered their weariness alone.

Through the small, smeared window he could see the burned-over stand of trees outside. The blackened arms in the half-light of dusk were tortured scarecrows that stretched and groaned in the late afternoon wind.

The train stopped at a small, unfenced cemetery dug in amidst the gnarled stumps of the fire-scarred hilltop. The few headstones were old, cheap and tilted. But higher up the hill, set apart from the rest, was a single, well-cared-for grave.

Adam Ward's wife, Brannon guessed. Even in death she would remain apart from the dust of the townspeople.

In the foreground was the open grave. Two men with shovels stood above it, waiting for the casket to fill the gaping hole.

The mourners got off the train like sleepwalkers. No one spoke. The men didn't even grunt as they bore the heavy casket from the flat car.

Only the dog made noise. He yapped at the sight of Alfie standing beside the cab of the train. A man's foot kicked the animal and even he was silent for a time.

While the others gathered at the open grave, Brannon walked alone to the top of the hill.

Catherine Ward followed him later. She caught up with him as he stood beside her mother's grave, his tall figure framed by a pair of arthritic, charred trees. When he noticed her, the wind was adding a touch of wildness to her hair. She was lovely, although the failing light was emphasizing the slight lines fanning out from the edges of her eyes.

"So soon the grave," he said, without thinking.

"What?" she asked.

"Nothing."

He put his hand to her neck. Her skin was soft and fresh. She put her hand over his and held it there. Then, gently, she brought it down from her neck.

"They can see," she said.

He looked down at the group around the grave and knew she was right.

"You're going to buy the stock from Cameron's widow, aren't you?" she said.

"Yes."

"Then what? Will you level Timberland?"

"Yes."

"But why?" Her furstration came through in her voice. "Are you destroying us for money? Is there some hidden profit?" He wanted to laugh, but he knew that would hurt her more than he needed. "Or is it somebody you want?" He looked at her more carefully and thought of all the nights he had wanted her, the nights he had relived their moments together, the way he had tried to recreate the feeling, not with his mind but with his body. And the sick, emptiness that always followed. "Is it Louise you want?" she asked. "Surely you can't belive she will go with you."

"You saw her with me at the tree?"

"She's a child mentally. She's old enough, but she doesn't understand men like you. Here in this dying town she's been isolated, a nun in her cloister. Our name is her habit."

"And you've told her nothing."

Catherine whirled away from him. Her voice came back to him bitterly. "What should I have told her? How a man can carry her to the heights, then smash her against the rocks? How he can give her ecstasy for a moment and hell for a lifetime?"

Brannon touched her again. It was her last chance, he knew. The town's last opportunity to survive. Just a slight warmth in his groin, a stirring, that's all he asked. When there was nothing, he lashed out, his tongue a knife that he hoped to slice across her belly.

"No," he said. "Tell her how to take a man, how to writhe in his arms, how to moan with pleasure . . . and then, how to scream for help when she thinks her precious name is at stake."

Above them, the clouds swirled and thunder rumbled in the distance. The first drop of rain struck her cheek, but she didn't notice.

"Why did you say that?" she asked incredulously. "What has that to do with you . . . with us?"

"Everything," he said. "A woman's scream . . . that's why I'm here. That's why Cameron died."

She stepped away from him. He saw fear in her eyes and he clutched at her arm. His grip was harsh and cruel.

"A girl who arched to meet me . . . matched me

thrust for thrust, then cried rape and called in a pack of animals . . . Cameron, Grossett, your father, even your sick, half-wit brother. They tore at me, using their hands like teeth."

Her face grew old before him. He thought she'd scream, but her gasp came out as a whisper.

"My God, it was you."

He told her, "Yes. I'm the kid . . . the soldier . . . the one with the laugh on his lips . . . the one women went for. . . ."

She tried to pry his fingers from her arms. She twisted her shoulder and strained against him.

"No, he was young. He loved me. Our hands touched and we knew."

His hands almost relaxed.

The fear started to fade from her eyes. Her voice grew tender again. She seemed to be speaking to someone else, someone not on the hill with them.

"Just a touch of our fingers. That couldn't be you."

Cruelly he pulled her into his arms. Their bodies touched, but he didn't kiss her. Behind them the wind rumbled. More rain pelted their flesh.

For a long time they stood together. Then gently she kissed him.

"You did come back," she said then. "But why?"

"For you," he told her, "and the one with the knife."

Puzzled, she raised her fingers to the scar on his cheek. "For this?"

"No. Because one of you cut me deeper . . . slashed me from the world." Roughly he shoved her aside and stepped away. He looked down at the people below. They weren't watching as he expected.

Their attention was fixed on the lowering casket. "I can't feel," he continued. "Can't hate properly, can't love. I'm an automaton pretending to be a man."

"You're talking in riddles again."

"A machine. Heartless metal that can't quit until the spring runs down. Leveling Timberland is just part of the program."

"Brannon, don't talk of that. Not now, please."

"When I'm through there'll be no town, no houses, no buildings left to show that it ever existed."

"Brannon, I've waited," she cried. "Honestly. I've planned . . . every word I'd say. For six thousand nights I practiced. I'd say I'm sorry. I shouldn't have screamed. I'd say, forgive me. I'd say. . . ."

"No, Catherine, none of that matters."

"But is does. A person can't live, not really live, not without a purpose. And all these years, thinking about you, waiting for you to come back, knowing you would. . . ."

Deliberately he cut her off with a wave of his hand. He had to say it fast before she shattered his resolve. "I've come to kill," he said. "One of you has to die . . . the one who came back for me that night . . . the one who came back with the knife, after the beating."

"I don't understand."

He turned away and started down the hill toward the grave. She called out to him, much as her daughter had done.

"Brannon," she cried.

From below came the sudden, shocking sound of the train whistle, not the playful tooting of before, but a shriek, a loud, painful, almost human wail.

The stunned mourners at the graveside froze as sitffly as the charred trees around them.

Alfie had come out of the train. His mouth gaped. His eyes were glassy. In front of him, his hands gripped the furry neck of the dog. The animal hung limp and silent, quite dead.

There was no pleasure in Alfie's face, as though the death of his tormentor had brought only bewilderment.

Solemnly he walked to the grave. The townspeople stepped aside to form an aisle. Like an altar boy bearing a glistening candelabra, he kept his eyes straight ahead.

He stopped, held out his arms, and let his fingers open. The corpse of the dog dropped into the grave.

A woman screamed. Another cried. The men turned away.

From the summit of the hill, Brannon moved downward. He knew Catherine was close behind him, but his attention was on Louise. She was running toward him, her arms outstretched. When she reached him, he folded her in against his chest and let her sob. "I'm not like him," she screamed. "Tell me, Brannon. I'm not like Alfie."

He comforted her with his arms, but he looked past her to Alfie.

The half-wit shrank back from his gaze as he come out from under the protective coating of his trance. "No," Alfie cried. "I didn't do it. I didn't.

He fell back. He stumbled. He bumped against the widow and crashed against someone else. He fled down the railroad track toward town, but he kept slipping, falling.

From the graveside, Adam Ward lashed out at Brannon. "Damn you, leave us alone."

Ward shoved through the small crowd and started after his son. When he caught him, he brought him back toward the train.

Almost alone now at the grave, Steve Grossett confronted Brannon. "Do as he says, Mr. Brannon," he warned. "Leave us before one of us has to kill you."

Quietly Steve Grossett joined the group moving to the train.

Only Louise and Brannon held back. Although the rain moistened their clothes and the wind chilled their faces, the girl tugged at his arm. "Let's not go with the others," she pleaded. "We could cut through the woods to your lake place."

When he tried to ignore her, she begged. "Don't go, please. Brannon, I'm afraid."

He paused. "Of what?" he asked.

"The town. They'll drive you away. They will. And when you're gone, it'll be worse than before. The same dead, stagnant emptiness; each of us . . . alive, but just waiting . . . waiting to take our place here on the hill. It's always been that way in Timberland, as long as I can remember . . . as though we died before we were born. We only wait to be buried. Then you came. At least you made them afraid."

Behind her the train whistle blew impatiently. Some of the men on the flatcar called. They cursed, their reverence wearing thin in the icy, jabbing rain.

"After you there'll be no hope," she said. "No dream. I couldn't bear that, not again."

Brannon studied her, realizing he had never

thought of her before. He had forgotten that she was a person, not just another structure in the decaying town.

He felt pity, almost savored the emotion, then squelched it quickly.

"It's time," he said aloud. "It's been too long. I'm weakening."

"What?" she asked.

He took her arm and led her past the hastily filled grave. "You want me to stay," he said. "Then help me get the stock I need."

Her muscles stiffened in his fingers. His directness had hurt her, but as he climbed into the caboose behind her, he felt the strength of confidence.

When the car lurched under him, he stood in the narrow aisle and took his checkbook from his pocket. He tore off the top one, holding it at eye level as he approached the widow.

"Mrs. Cameron," he said. "Sell now. Or never."

The fat woman quivered. Her hand raised hesitantly.

Around her the heads of the townspeople raised stiffly. None of their eyes moved, nor their mouths, but the woman's Adam's apple worked under the heavy folds of her neck.

From across the caboose, Grossett spoke to her. His voice was gentle, coaxing. "Don't, Mrs. Cameron. He wants to level the town."

"Think, Emma," Adam Ward cried. "It's your home too."

The fat woman glanced about, first at the men and then across the aisle at Catherine. The pudgy hand quivered again and began to withdraw.

"Sell the stock, Emma."

The voice of Louise Grossett rose above the rattling and the clanking of the rolling train.

Brannon looked at her first. He thought he could see the childish illusions fading fast from her youthful face. A child was dying, he thought vaguely. A woman takes her place.

The others looked toward her then. They wore expressions of mild surprise. They had never seen her before, he thought.

"Sell the stock," she said again. "If you don't, I'll sell mine."

"Louise!" her mother shouted.

Across the aisle, Adam Ward stiffened to his feet. His eyes appeared to bug out perceptibly. He seemed to be holding his breath.

"Darling," he said. "You wouldn't."

He clutched at his granddaughter and years of frustration burst out in her scream.

"Don't call me that," she yelled. She whipped his hand away and turned her face aside. "Don't touch me, now or ever."

Adam Ward's voice was weak and pathetic. "But, Louise, you can't. . . ."

Brannon pushed the old man aside and again held out the check to the widow.

"Now or never," he repeated.

The woman's hand closed on the check. As she took it from him, he thought he saw her smile, just a little.

CHAPTER 16

The eye-like headlight of the train jabbed at the darkness, making the pelting rain sparkle like pellets of fire hurtling down across the glistening rails. The thunder cracked, then rumbled, then cracked again. The wind came in gusts, spanking at the tree with a punishing fury.

In the town old signs flopped on rusted hinges, and doors to deserted buildings beat against their casements. Rotted boards groaned and mud-darkened puddles added a rhythm of raindrops splatting against their cratered surfaces.

The old cars parked near the crumbling depot glimmered briefly in the short white glare of the lightning, but as the train approached, only the door to the Mercedes opened. In a trench coat with his black head bare to the rain, Andrew Ledger stepped out and stood near the fender.

Brannon's secretary said something to him from the back seat of the car, but he didn't hear her. He hardly noticed the rain either. His thoughts were on the train. He felt foolish, but he was afraid for Brannon. He didn't know why, but he was afraid.

When the train stopped, he took a second coat from the car and crossed to the tracks. The townspeople climbing from the flat car and the caboose ignored him. They kept their heads down and leaned into the prickling rain, yet when they reached their cars, they hesitated. A few pretended to stay behind to say farewell again to the widow, but he knew there was more. They were watching the caboose, waiting.

He saw Louise. She came out running, and from the hunched position of her shoulders, he guessed she was crying. She ran toward the lead car of the procession, but Ledger put out his hand and caught her to him.

She stared up at him and in a flare of lightning he saw her face distorted with hurt and anger. Brannon has done something to her, he thought, something cruel.

"Let me go," she said, and for a moment he remembered his childhood, the first time he had ever touched a white girl. She had said the same thing, used the same tone.

His hand dropped away from her shoulder, but she didn't leave.

"What happened?" he asked. "Where's Brannon? Is he all right?"

She raised her hand and pointed at the caboose where Brannon was coming down into the rain. "There," she said. "He got what he wanted."

"The stock?"

"Yes. At a funeral. He made his deal. Now you can strip us all."

She ran to the lead car as Brannon approached.

Ledger handed the coat to his boss and helped him fold it across his shoulders. "You get what you want?" he said.

Brannon said, "Yes. You can settle the transfer details with Mrs. Cameron."

The white man crossed to the Mercedes and Ledger held the door for him. But Brannon leaned down, speaking to his secretary in the back seat without getting in. "Call the contractors," he said over the chatter of the rain. "Tell them I want equipment by noon. Cranes, dozers, at least a dozen men."

Marcia's voice sounded confused. "Noon tomorrow?" she asked.

Andrew Ledger came close. He pushed at his boss' shoulder. "You can't assume control that fast," he insisted. "There has to be a board meeting. A vote."

Brannon's tone was as cold as the rain. "Do as you're told," he ordered.

Ledger clenched his fist and felt his eyes narrowing like an animal ready to fight. "But they'll get an injunction," he argued. "Any court will grant a temporary restraining order until. . . ."

"That's my worry."

Brannon's hand came up and rested gently on the black man's shoulder. His tone softened. "Now get out of sight, Andy," he suggested. "There may be trouble."

Ledger wanted to curse. Damn Brannon anyway, he thought. What was he up to now?

Marcia sensed his concern and almost cried at their boss. "You're not staying behind?" she said. "Not alone?"

Brannon laughed. "It's my town now. I own it."

Ledger scoffed. "Sure, and your fellow citizens are angry enough to lynch you."

"Good. I want them mad. I want to create a rage that consumes them all. And I want you to settle things with Mrs. Cameron before someone changes her mind."

"Okay, boss, but I got a hunch that in the morning we're going to find you walking around dead."

Brannon laughed again, then turned away. As he stepped from the car, Ledger watched him go.

He stood in the blowing rain, the lightning cracking just beyond the building, the thunder booming with a threatening roar, the mud oozing up over the instep of his shoes, yet he couldn't bring himself to slip into the warm comfort of the car. Instead he watched as the people drifted to their cars, and he saw Alfie Ward breaking at the sight of Brannon and sprinting down the center of the rain-swept street into the darkness.

He saw Adam Ward and Grossett catching up with Louise and joining her in the shelter of the front car. Then, like everyone else in town, he saw Catherine Ward coming alone from the caboose.

She walked slowly, completely indifferent to rain dripping from the hem of her dress, although she held her hat down tightly on her head to protect her hair. In front of everyone she walked directly to Brannon. The others saw her through the blurring veil of rain as she stepped close to him, but Andrew Ledger heard what she said. Only he heard her, but he didn't understand.

"I loved you, Brannon," she said. "All these years, I loved you."

CHAPTER 17

Brannon felt cold. His wet clothing clung to his flesh like elastic socks, and icy rivulets ran down his back beneath his shirt. The wind stung his face and he shivered with every flash of lightning. Yet with the thunder roaring in his ears, he thought of a warm summer night when the air was still and gentle.

He remembered Catherine as he had seen her then, so young, so fresh, the few blemishes of youth hidden in the dimness of the moonlight. He recalled shaking too, then, all his cocksureness fading fast when he felt her hand so soft in his.

". . . all these years," she was saying again through the rain.

He nodded, trying to tell her he understood.

"You stood alone at night by the tree," he said. "That ugly, lovely tree . . . that's what your daughter calls it."

"She told you?"

"Yes."

Catherine came closer and he looked past her shoulder. The streaks of rain blurred the shadows, but he could tell. The people of the town were watching. He was on a stage, playing out a script only he understood. He couldn't weaken now.

He stepped away from her and walked toward the

center of the street, his big frame bent into the wind.

"I thought you'd come back," Catherine shouted after him.

He heard her sloshing along behind him, but he didn't stop until he reached the center of town and the blurred light of the grocery. He stepped onto the porch and waited for her as the townspeople finally began to pile into their cars. A few drove off, cutting close in front of the porch, but others parked back near the depot, their car lights still on, waiting, yet afraid to come closer.

Only Catherine came to the porch, and she stood at the far end where the rain could still reach her.

"I thought you'd come back," she said again.

"I did," he told her.

"That's not what I mean. I thought you wanted me. I thought you came back for me."

"I can have your daughter. She's half your age."

He couldn't see her face even when the lightning flared between the buildings, but he knew he had hurt her. He had wanted that once, he thought. For years he had wanted to see her in pain, to know she shared his agony.

But now he didn't want to see the effect of his words. He left the porch and went back out into the rain. He nearly fell in the slimy street, and the storm roared with new fury as though his brazenness insulted the wind. Still, Catherine came along beside him, her hands clutching at him to hold him back.

"Louise?" she shouted. "That's the one thing you can't have. Not the way you mean, not as a woman."

He smirked at her cruelly. "She'd go to bed with me anytime. Ask her?"

"No. But you can have the town. You bought it.

But not Louise. Not ever." She clutched his arm tighter and brought her rain-streaked face close to his. "Take me instead. I've waited."

He sneered. "Like I said. Show me what I'm getting."

She faded back, covering her mouth with a hand, and he left her again.

At the next doorway, he stopped. Boards nailed across broken glass barred the door, but the faded paint still bore the words, "Soda Fountain." And he imagined he remembered the store as it must have been that night, its windows bright with light, its door open to catch the summer breeze, and from within, the high-pitched buzz of a malted milk being whipped into a creamy thickness.

"Damn," he said.

He reared back and kick with one foot. The cross boards splintered and the door swung open. Spreading his hands before his face to sweep away the spider webs, he went inside.

In the dim light he could see the toadstool shapes of the backless seats along the counter and he could make out the handles to the soft drink dispensers, but the room lacked the scrubbed clean smell of a fountain; instead it stank of dust and rotting wood.

He went in farther, the linoleum crackling under his feet. A chair toppled when he touched it, and he stumbled against a nearly empty rack of magazines. The pages crumbled like dried leaves, and the swivel rack grated as he spun it.

He was searching. What for, he didn't know. Still he was resentful when Catherine's voice interrupted him from the street door.

"Is this what you wanted to see?" she was asking.

She closed the door and stood just inside. She unbuttoned her coat and let it fall at her feet. Then she raised her hands to the buttons of her blouse. She made a movement with her arms and the blouse joined the coat on the floor.

The bra came next. She unlatched it quickly and dropped it along with the other clothes.

A flash of lightning revealed she was naked from the waist, but the brief, brilliant flare was behind her and he saw nothing of what he wanted to see. So he took his lighter from his pocket and held it out between them. When the flame was full size, he could see the breasts were large and firm, quite erect too. But the nipples were still soft, although they heaved upward with every breath she took.

The skirt came just to her navel, and her stomach was flat, almost concave under the bottom row of ribs. He could tell where her hips would start to flare outward and he could guess approximately how far beneath her navel his hand would have to reach before it found the soft rectangle of hair.

But he couldn't recall the feeling he'd had when he'd first put his hand there so many years before. Where had it begun? In the hand itself? Or in his groin? Or was there a hot flush in the cheeks first before his heart began to thump faster?

He willed his heart to beat faster. He wanted his face to feel hot. He demanded that the flesh of his groin grow riled and seethe with lust.

Instead he screamed in rage. The back of his hand whipped across her face and knocked her back against the rotting table behind her. The lighter flicked out in his hand, but he could see the wire magazine rack tumble on top of her.

Still he couldn't stop himself. His foot caught a chair and kicked it against the wall. Another sweep of his hand cleared several glasses from the counter where they had sat for years. He drove his fist into a dust-caked jar and sprayed the room with splintered glass and and the black crumbs of long-rotten cones.

"You bitch," he cried. "You filthy bitch."

In the darkness he stumbled through the room, breaking anything that he touched. The mirrors behind the counter cracked and slipped out of place. Fixtures fell or bent before his flaying arms. Through it all, he shouted, words even he didn't understand.

Then, as quickly as it had come, the rage subsided, and he sank on his knees to the floor. He felt Catherine's arm and pushed the magazine rack aside. He pulled her into a sitting position and brought her against his chest.

She was crying.

He put his hands behind her neck and brought her face up to his. He kissed her.

She clutched at him frantically.

Instantly he wanted to push her away. Instead he tried to kiss her again, hard, with an angry passion that he remembered from another world.

"Oh, mother!"

The words shocked him. And he looked up, realizing the wind and rain were lashing at them through the open door again.

Louise's silhouette stood there.

Catherine thrust him away. She clambered to her feet and tried to clutch her blouse across her chest.

"Louise," she gasped.

The girl didn't move and he couldn't see her face,

but he could see she was staring at her mother's naked breasts.

Catherine slipped the blouse onto her arms and tried to button it. But when her daughter turned back toward the door, she started after her, shouting her name.

She darted out into the rain and Brannon followed. At the curb he stopped. He could see the girl as she stumbled down the street into the arms of her grandfather. The old man held her momentarily, then she shook loose and disappeared into the darkness.

Catherine didn't try to follow. She waited as Adam Ward approached. Beside him came Alfie, his railman's lantern turning the rain into a spray of tiny, sparkling meteorites that formed a thin veil between them.

"Catherine, what is it?" Adam Ward called. "What's happening?"

"It's him, father," Catherine cried over the wind. "The soldier. He's back."

"I told you, Pa," Alfie screamed. "It is him. He come back to kill us."

He raised his lantern and the old man cocked his head for a better look.

"You did come back," he said, and his voice was weak with sadness.

Brannon stepped toward them, then saw the shotgun in the shaking hands of the old man. Its double barrel pointed squarely at his head.

"Stay there," Ward ordered.

When Brannon moved again, the gun barrel raised deliberately, then spit out flame. The cluster of pellets shattered glass back of his head and instinctively he hunched his shoulders. Yet he didn't retreat.

He thought of the days in the war. His head buzzed and his ears rang as they did then when the shells fell near him. Only in those days he had feared death. Now he feared only the pain that came first.

"Kill him, Pa," Alfie begged. "Kill him."

But the older man stepped back, aiming the gun at his target again, but his voice no longer strong. "Why now, Brannon?" he whined. "After all these years."

Brannon took the gun from him. He pushed the barrel aside, yanked the weapon from Ward's hand, and flung it away. Then his fist knocked the old man to his knees.

Alfie crouched on the street beside his father. With the rain dripping from their faces, they cowered together.

"I came back because you're dying, old man," Brannon told them. "Or haven't they told you yet?"

Briefly he felt the satisfaction of revenge. He remembered the night they had helped beat him to the ground. But he had fought back. The old man before him now was too sick to care.

"You came to tell me that?" Ward asked.

"Yes," Brannon answered. "And to watch you die. I want to be here; to tell you over and over. It's time. Your time to die."

"Brannon," Catherine whispered.

Her voice surprised him. He had almost forgotten she still stood just a yard away.

"Don't hurt him," she pleaded. "He's old and sick. It's me you hate."

She touched his arm and he shoved her away.

Then he heard her husband calling from down the street. "Catherine, leave him alone. He's crazy."

She ran to him, and Brannon realized that some of the townspeople still hovered in the background.

With the darkness hampering his vision, with the gusting rain blurring the sight of her, he could only guess that she wept as Grossett wrapped his arms around her. But the sudden loneliness he felt was almost overwhelming.

A nightmare that had haunted him for twenty years flashed across his mind.

Catherine naked. Catherine pressed against a man. Catherine moaning as he entered her.

In his sleep the nightmare had driven him awake with rage. A thousand times he had come to in the darkness of his room, his body bathed in perspiration, his fists clenched in anger.

But tonight the thought only made him lonely.

Then he saw her leave her husband's arms and run down the street toward the house.

With her gone, he could look back down at the men before him. And anger again replaced the loneliness.

"You came back for me," Ward was saying. "For beating you that night? Is that it?"

"Yes," Brannon replied. "And for Alfie too."

He yanked the half-wit to his feet. Alfie shuddered and dropped the lantern. He stumbled to the porch of the grocery.

"Pa, help me," he cried. "I'll be good. Honest, Pa. Only don't let him beat me."

Brannon picked up the lantern and held it high. He started to the porch, but the old man, his clothes and hands smeared with mud, climbed up out of the street and tried to block him.

"What do you want with Alfie?" he asked. "He's only a shell of a man."

"Like Timberland," Brannon told him. "A ghost town. I could never figure out why. But you could tell me, couldn't you, Alfie? You know what happened here. You know why a bustling town suddenly had to die."

"What's he sayin', Pa?" Alfie whimpered. "What's he mean?"

Terrified, Alfie flattened himself against the building wall. And as he stepped back, his hand touched the old wooden rocker still on the porch. Given momentum it creaked back and forth eerily in the wind. Alfie stared at it as a man stares at a coiled snake.

Brannon held the lantern above the chair, blocking it from the wind with his body. But still it rocked, slowly, methodically.

"You remember Sid Webster, Alfie," Brannon told him. "Used to sit in that chair, rocking. All the time, rocking."

Alfie shook his head.

"Sure, you remember, Alfie."

The half-wit's mouth formed words. "No, no." But the sound didn't come out above the wind and the lashing rain.

"Used to make bets, crazy bets with people. You remember him."

"What the hell you trying to do, Brannon?" Adam Ward asked.

He stumbled to the porch and tried to place himself between Brannon and his son.

"Leave him alone. Take your revenge on me."

Ignoring him, Brannon closed in on the quivering shape along the wall.

"You knew Webster, Alfie. You killed him. Remember? And you hid his body, right?"

Alfie screamed. His chest heaved out the cry like a deep breath held far too long.

He shoved himself from the wall. His arms shadowboxed the air. He screamed again and spun around. Then he fell from the porch, flailed about in the mud and crawled into the street. When he stood up again, he ran into the night.

Brannon moved to go after him.

"Please, let him go," Adam Ward pleaded. "He's got the mind of a child."

"He's a killer."

"You don't know that."

Brannon stepped into the rain and Adam Ward hobbled after him.

"Sid Webster's not dead," Ward insisted. "Not as far as we know. He left town. That's all. Years ago. He had no family, no friends."

"He's dead. Alfie killed him. It figures."

"There's no proof of that. Not even a body. You have to have a body."

Brannon stopped. He thought he saw a movement in the darkness.

Crossing the street he stood before the broken candy-striped sign of the deserted barber shop. He tried the door and it swung open ahead of him.

He left the rain and entered another deserted room. The windows of the shop were caked with dirt, but they let in the occasional flash of lightning, and he could see that nothing remained but the three empty barber chairs. All neatly turned in the same direction, he could almost imagine three men sitting there, the white striped cloths covering them to their necks, and three barbers, their hands poised at shoulder height, their scissors ready to snip.

Obviously Alfie wasn't in the barren cubicle and he went out into the rain again. Adam Ward trailed along with him, his old body buffeted by the slashing wind, as Brannon searched the empty building. Behind them the rest of the townspeople climbed in their cars and drove towards home.

By the time they neared the billiard parlor with its sagging tables and broken cues, Brannon realized someone had searched the buildings before. And often. In some places walls had been ripped out. In all of them closet doors and cabinets stood open.

He thought he knew who had preceded him.

"Brannon, wait," Ward begged.

This time the old man blocked the door with his body.

"Any of us could have killed Webster," he said suddenly. His voice cracked. He seemed ready to cry. "He was going to tell Catherine . . . about you . . . about the bet."

Brannon slumped against the door frame. The strength flowed out of his shoulders.

He felt the sharp jab of remorse.

What if Catherine had found out the truth, he thought. What if she learned she was only the prize in a wager? A cheap wager between stupid, insensitive men stinking with beer and cheap whiskey.

He'd have killed the man, too, he knew that. But it changed nothing.

"It doesn't matter," he shouted.

He straightened his shoulders and crossed the street to the movie theater.

Behind the broken glass of the display cases the faded posters still advertised the last film shown. "High Noon." Price, thirty cents. Inside he held the lantern high and looked down on the empty rows of seats. At the front the beaded screen hung in shreds.

"The night Webster disappeared, Alfie must have seen something," Ward said from behind him.

"Like where the body was hidden," Brannon suggested as he moved slowly through the theater, probing beneath the seats with the light from the lantern.

"Alfie . . . he keeps trying to remember. He rips out walls, and roots in the earth."

Brannon turned and looked up the aisle at the older man. In the glare from the lantern, the wrinkles on Ward's face were deep black furrows. His eyes squinted and he held a hand defensively in front of him.

"So you closed down the town," Brannon said. "You closed the mill, the stores, the theater, everything you could. To keep someone from finding the truth."

Ward shivered. "What else could I do? One of us may be a murderer. One of us might have killed Webster. Maybe his body is here somewhere, buried, or stuffed behind some junk."

Ward sank into a chair. He bent over, burying his face in his hands. When he spoke again, his voice was muffled. "Just the thought of it drove my wife to suicide."

"Tough," Brannon said, then regretted his callousness. Ward's wife wasn't involved. She'd done nothing to him. Yet she was dead, an innocent victim of that night.

He started to say, "I'm sorry." But the words didn't feel natural and instead he walked farther down the aisle toward the screen.

"Brannon," Ward called to him. "Let it lie."

Brannon stopped, keeping his back to the older man.

"It's the only way."

"No," Brannon told him. "You bastards beat me that night. Now you pay."

"By finding Webster?" Ward asked skeptically. "By finding his dry bones, his rotting flesh? That's how you pay us back."

"Yes."

"But who? Who do you repay?"

"You."

"And Alfie?"

"Yes."

"Steve too?"

"Of course."

"Why Steve? Because he married Catherine? He was against the bet. Remember? He came for me. He tried to stop you."

"Him too," Brannon answered coldly. "The whole damned town. You all pay."

"Brannon, you don't understand." Ward raised his head and sat erect in the seat. He made his voice as clear and distinct as possible when he spoke again. "It could have been Catherine." He paused and ran his hand to his forehead. He seemed ready to vomit. "Maybe she found out about the bet. Maybe she killed Webster."

CHAPTER 18

Brannon felt a wave of panic sweep over him. He hadn't thought of Catherine as a killer.

But before he could consider the possibilty, he saw another shadow enter the theater. With the lantern held higher he could make out the figure of Steve Grossett.

Strange, he thought, here was the one man from that night who had never seemed important. A weak shadow figure in the background, and yet here was Catherine's husband, the man she must have slept with through these years, the man who had taken the place he had always wanted.

"Come on, Adam," Grossett was saying. "Let's get out of here."

He came down the aisle and helped his father-in-law from his seat.

"Steve," Ward whined. "You have to stop Brannon. He's hunting for Alfie. Tracking him like an animal. Trying to make him talk. You have to stop him."

"I'm taking you home first."

"But he'll keep searching . . . just like Alfie. Hunting. Probing. Digging."

"Not for long," Grossett answered, and the vehemence in his voice was surprising.

Then they were gone. They walked up the aisle together and disappeared into the raging storm.

Alone Brannon moved down to the front of the theater. When he stopped, he realized he wasn't alone after all. He could hear the sounds . . . grunting noises like an animal rooting in the earth.

Before him hung the tattered remnants of the screen. When he tried to push it aside, it collapsed, falling from the ceiling in an exploding cloud of dust.

Through the cloud, Alfie Ward leaped. With his arms spread-eagle, he flew at Brannon, missed, and crashed into the front row of seats.

The half-wit's face twisted in an agony of its own as he floundered on the floor, beating the threadbare carpeting with his fists until he staggered upright and stumbled up the aisle toward the exit.

"Did you find it, Alfie?" Brannon shouted after him. He went up the aisle behind him, egging him on with his taunts. "Webster's body, that's what you're looking for. Remember, Alfie? The body. . . ."

In the street the rain came straight down in drenching torrents, but Alfie didn't appear to notice. He stood in the center of the road, his arms outstretched, twirling slowly.

With a sudden conviction, he darted for the door of the old auditorium. He was inside before Brannon came out of the theater. The swinging door gave him away.

Before he followed, Brannon searched the street. He was alone again. At least he could see no one, and the only visible light came from the lantern in his hand.

When he reached the auditorium, he entered cautiously. The outer lobby was empty and he could hear the grunting noises coming from the main part of the hall. There were other noises too, loud cracking sounds like chairs being tossed against a wall, then the sharp twang of piano strings as an angry fist pounded the keyboard.

He went through the second set of doors and squinted into the huge cavern of a room. In the center of the dance floor, Alfie Ward whirled blindly. Like a child spinning himself dizzy, he twirled drunkenly, kicking and hitting at the folding chairs that hampered his movements.

When the light pierced the darkness, he covered his eyes with the crook of his elbow and stopped his weird little dance. His lips pulsated, trying to speak. The sound that came out, though, was the sound of a train whistle, a child's imitation.

"Toot, toot," he moaned mournfully.

"Hello, Alfie," Brannon said. "Is this the place?"

Alfie stepped back. He tooted again, weaker this time.

"Show me," Brannon told him. "Show me where it is, Alfie."

"No," Alfie whispered. "I don't knew nothin'. Ain't seen nothin'."

"Sure you have . . . you remember."

The lantern came closer. He retreated, whimpering. He'd tried to make the tooting sounds again, but he blubbered. Saliva spilled from the corner of his mouth.

"No, don't knew nothin'. Nothin' at all. Nothin', you hear?"

Then suddenly he dopped the arm from across his eyes. He stared into the lantern. He groaned.

His shoulders slumped and he turned away. He

walked stiffly to the back of the room, hesitated at the rusted guard railing around a circular staircase, then started down into the basement. He mumbled to himself as he went.

Brannon stood at the top of the staircase for a time, letting the lantern shed its light into the basement.

When he heard the anguished moan, he went down.

Alfie stood in front of the huge old coal furnace, his back to the stairs. He was moaning as he opened the furnace door. He probed inside, then straightened up again and turned.

Brannon held the lantern out ahead of him, letting it bathe the blackened furnace in its cold, raw light. He looked down at Alfie.

Alfie held out the objects in front of him . . . the dried bones of a human hand.

Now it was Brannon who groaned. He felt sick inside. Through the open door of the furnace he could see other bones protruding from the caked mat of ashes.

"Webster," he said to himself.

Alfie's reaction to the name was violent. He cried out and flung the thing in his hands at the floor. He bolted for the staircase, knocking Brannon against the railing.

The lantern smashed against the basement wall. The glass shattered and flames flared up around Brannon's hand. Instinctively, he tossed it away from his body. It hit the floor and exploded with a gentle puffing sound. Tongues of fire squirted out into a stack of folding chairs.

Brannon grabbed for Alfie, but the frightened

half-wit knocked him aside and escaped up the staircase. For another moment, Brannon tried to fight the flames. He ripped off his wet coat and beat at the fire. With an almost human rage, they raced to consume the wood. The heat burned his face and the smoke gagged him.

With his eyes streaked with tears, he retreated up the stairs, the flames licking at him from behind. By the time he reached the main floor, the staircase was a roaring chimney. Already flickering light showed through the cracks in the rotting floor of the stage; he could feel the heat through the soles of his shoes.

Gasping for breath, he stumbled across the dance floor. Then he stopped abruptly as he saw the shape of a man standing just inside the exit.

Smoke blurred his vision. He couldn't make out the face. But he could see the hand extended in front of the body. He could see the pistol pointed at him.

Brannon saw the spit of flame from the gun. He felt something powerful grab his sleeve and spin him around. He felt the hot burning streak across his shoulder, but he didn't hear the crack of the bullet.

He dropped to the floor and rolled.

Another bullet plunked into the floor beside him. A third slashed past his ear.

He fell back into the flames now coming up through the floor of the stage. His wet clothes sizzled and his eyeballs smarted from the heat. With geysers of fire waist-high around him, he couldn't tell if the man with the gun was still shooting.

Whipping his arm ahead of him, he plunged through the flames to the back of the stage and found the exit he had hoped for. The brass knob of the door burned his hand, but refused to budge. He kicked frantically at the panel . . . once, twice, three times before the door swung open.

He stumbled out into the cool drizzle. It felt good on his skin, but he didn't pause. He hurried away from the building, hiding himself in the darkness. He didn't stop until he reached the railroad tracks. There he leaned against the black steel of Alfie's railroad engine.

From his hiding place he could see the townspeople coming out into the street, forming a sparse ring around the burning auditorium. A few tried to fight it, scampering about with buckets of water, hauling garden hoses from the spigots of nearby buildings, but most of them only watched as the fire became a Christmas tree of flames spearing at the blackened sky.

As he breathed in the welcomed fresh air, Brannon ran his hand to his wounded shoulder. It came away bloody, but he could tell it wasn't serious. The greater danger lay behind him in the streets of the town.

Somewhere there stood the man who had tried to kill him, the man with the gun.

Who? he wondered.

Adam Ward? The crazy Alfie? Or Grossett? Possibly even Catherine. Maybe he had only thought it was a man.

But one of them was a killer. One of them couldn't afford to let him live, not after what he had seen in the basement furnace.

But who?

CHAPTER 19

In the cool light of dawn, the townspeople picked through the charred wreckage of the auditorium. They lifted fallen beams and kicked at the stacks of rubble with their feet. The rain had stopped, but their clothes were stained from the black pools of water that had formed on the exposed flooring.

Andrew Ledger stood in the street and watched. He had chosen not to poke around the ruins and no one had challenged him except Marcia. She stood behind him, pouting.

"Do something," she said more than once. "Help them or call the sheriff. But don't just stand there."

He ignored her, holding back and leaving the dirty work to the others. He didn't know why. He just didn't seem to belong there among the wreckage of the collapsed roof and the tilting walls.

When he saw Steve Grossett coming out of the ruins, he went over to him. "Found anything yet?" he asked.

Grossett shook his head. "Nothing yet. But they're searching the basement now."

From several steps away, Marcia spoke painfully. "He can't be dead. Not Brannon."

Grossett shrugged. "We saw him go in, just before the fire. Only Alfie came out."

He started to say more, but a lean man in a smoke-smudged jacket called to him from the stack of timbers near the back of the auditorium.

"Mr. Grossett."

The man came out of the rubble carrying the twisted remains of a lantern.

"Steve, what did you find?" Catherine called from the open door of her car. With her daughter Louise behind her, she ran across the street to her husband. Adam Ward, hobbling from fatigue, joined them.

"Alfie's lantern," Grossett told her. "Brannon had it with him the last time anyone saw him alive."

Only Louise registered horror. "Oh, mother, that poor man."

Adam Ward, though, grunted approval. "He had it coming. The bastard."

"Damn you," Marcia cursed.

Tears of frustration formed in her eyes, but the sudden rumbling sound behind them distracted her. Like the others, she turned.

Around the corner came the brightly painted demolition equipment, a huge bulldozer and a small wrecking crane both riding on the flat bed trailer of a diesel truck. It rumbled up the street and airbraked to a stop a few yards from the theater. The driver and another man climbed down from the cab. They looked confused.

"Mr. Brannon ordered the equipment," Marcia explained. "He wanted it here first thing this morning."

"He intended to start razing the town today," Ledger added.

Adam Ward snorted, "The maniac."

Steve Grossett found a cigarette and put it to his

mouth. He lit it. "Brannon won't be taking control now," he said. He faced the equipment operators and told them they wouldn't be needed after all. The men stared at him blankly.

Then Andrew Ledger stepped forward, his black face knotted by determination. "The hell they won't," he said.

"But Brannon's dead," Grossett protested. "He. . . ."

"Is he?

Ledger turned and faced the men from the truck. "Get the equipment off the truck. Start here," he said, making a motion toward the burned out auditorium. "Clear it out, then move on to the next building and the next. Don't stop until I tell you."

"Don't be a fool," Grossett warned him.

The men shrugged. They went back to the truck and began unloading the dozer. They had it on the street when the train whistle shrieked from near the depot.

It didn't toot this time. It wailed, long and loud and mournfully—like a dog baying at the moon.

From the street, the people near the auditorium could see the cab of the engine. Alfie hung from the open window. His eyes were open but his face was expressionless. If there were any thoughts left in his mind, it was no longer obvious.

In between the train and the small crowd stood the other man. His injured arm hung limply at his side. His face was smudged and bruised, his clothing blackened from the fire. But when he walked toward them, his eyes bore the rigid determination of a gunfighter.

"Brannon, you're alive," Louise Ward cried.

She ran to him, throwing herself against his chest. She sobbed and he put an arm around her, but he kept coming. "You're not dead," she screamed. "Thank God. Thank God."

She walked with him, his arm across her shoulders.

Ledger made a motion toward the rubble with his head. "We thought you were in there. Grossett said he saw you."

Brannon ignored the others. He stared at Catherine. For a moment the girl at his side thought he was deserting her again.

"You came back for me," Louise cried. "Not her. Tell me. You're going to take me away with you. Tell them all. I want them to hear." When he hesitated, her fists beat at his chest. "Tell them," she screamed. "We're going away together."

Adam Ward came forward.

"Leave her alone, Brannon. You're not doing to her what you did to her mother."

Brannon sneered. "You going to stop me, old man?"

"If I have to."

Ward reached into the back seat of his car. When he straightened up again he held the shotgun he had used the night before. He tried to aim it at Brannon.

"Don't, father," Catherine yelled. "You'll hit Louise."

Brannon pushed the girl aside. He stood alone in front of the gun as Ward cocked the trigger.

He aimed but his son-in-law leaped forward to pull the gun from his hands.

"Kill him," Ward cried. "Kill him before he takes Louise from us."

Grossett shook his head. "He can't take her." He laughed. "He's not capable of. . . ."

He stopped in mid-sentence.

Brannon and he stared at each other. Only they seemed to exist. For a moment only they understood.

"You!" Brannon whispered. "You know!"

Grossett stepped backward. His hands quivered. The gun seemed to give him no courage.

"Get away from me, Brannon," he cried. "I'll kill you." But still he held the gun high, not aiming. Instead he backed away toward the rubble.

"You're the one," Brannon snarled. "You're the one who came back that night . . . the one with the knife."

Louise looked at her father. She saw how the gun shook in his hand. "Father," she cried. "What's he mean? What's he saying?" She put out a hand, but he motioned her away.

"Don't come near me," Grossett yelled. "You're no daughter of mine."

Louise stopped, not quite certain what she had heard. Her mother came to her side, but didn't touch her.

Her grandfather moved closer too, but he spoke to Grossett. "Steve, do you know what you're saying?"

"Damn you," Catherine cursed.

Then Brannon stepped menacingly toward the man with the gun. "Tell them, you bastard. Tell them the truth before I kill you."

Grossett smirked. "Is that what you want, Brannon. You want me to to tell Catherine why I helped raise her child . . . why I never touched her in all these years."

Brannon felt dizzy. His eyes smarted again like they had from the heat in the fire.

"You lie," he said.

Grossett shook his head again. "No. What I did to you with a knife, I did to myself with regret." His voice lowered. He seemed to be talking to himself. "I'm not the only one. It's the whole town. We all died that night, and now you want to bury us."

Brannon said, "Yes. When I'm done there won't be a single stone left in Timberland, not a building, not even the outline of a house, nothing to show that any of you ever lived. You stole my immortality. Now I'll have yours."

He made a motion toward the rubble of the burned-out auditorium. "And we'll start right here. We'll clean away the wreckage and show the town what you've got down in that basement."

Brannon walked to the bulldozer and climbed up to its seat.

"Hey, careful there, mister," the operator shouted. "You'll get yourself hurt."

Brannon waved him away as he turned on the engine. "Get out of here. I pay the bills."

The dozer groaned and moved forward.

"No," Grossett shouted. "That's one thing you'll never do."

He whirled, pointing the gun toward Louise.

"Not unless you want to see your own daughter die. You hear me, Brannon? She's yours . . . not mine . . . the only child you'll ever have."

But the bulldozer creaked ahead. Its huge blade lifted and shoved toward Grossett at chest level. For a moment he aimed at the girl, then changed his mind and whirled toward Brannon. He fired, but the pellets clattered harmlessly against the scoop blade racing forward.

He pulled the second trigger, but the hammer clicked against a spent shell. Then the blade struck. He grunted as it cut into his body.

The dozer stopped and he slipped free. For an instant he gaped at his innards as they spilled out on the street.

He was dead by the time Brannon had leaped from the controls of the dozer.

Brannon felt nothing as he looked down at the gore. There was no sense of satisfaction, only the sadness that comes at the end of a day.

He hardly realized others were still there. They formed a silent semi-circle a dozen paces back. Only Adam Ward came close enough to stand where the blood could reach his shoes. And he whispered, so the others couldn't hear.

"It's over," he said.

But Brannon said. "No. There are ashes in the basement. Webster's ashes."

The feeble old man at his side nodded. "I know. I figured as much from Alfie's babbling. That was probably Steve's doing too. He hated Webster for his part in the bet. But it doesn't matter."

"The truth has to be told."

"What truth?" Ward asked. "That your daughter was conceived on a bet, a practical joke among a bunch of beer-drinking bums? Or would you rather tell Catherine that she waited a lifetime . . . hungering for the man who deflowered her, all for a few laughs and a lift out of town? Tell them that and

I'll know Steve did more than castrate you. I'll know he stole your soul."

Brannon turned away from the body. He faced the ring of people and they avoided his eyes.

He saw Louise. She stood with Andrew Ledger, her face against the black man's shoulder.

"Andy, take Louise home," Brannon ordered gently.

Louise raised her head to protest. "But I don't want to. . . ."

"Later," he told her. "We'll talk."

Then he searched the small crowd for Catherine. When he didn't see her, his secretary seemed to understand.

Marcia said, "She's gone. I don't know where."

Brannon sighed. "I'll find her," he said.

He passed through the group, heading up the street, walking slowly at first, then faster, almost running. He was afraid, he realized. For the first time in years. He was afraid she'd be gone.

He found her where he knew she'd be, by the tree, the ugly, gnarled tree. She stood with her back to him. She looked out over the dried-up millpond, across the marshy spaces toward the wreckage of the deserted mill. She didn't turn even when he spoke.

"You understand now?" he asked.

"What he did to you?" she said. "Yes. I understand now." She whirled, facing him hopefully. "But there must be ways . . . doctors, operations . . . I thought they could help."

"They can," he agreed. "Sometimes. They tried with me. I got rich trying to earn enough to pay the doctors. But nothing worked. Not with me. So there was no point in coming back."

"Except hate."

"I came to think I couldn't even hate," he said. "I felt numb—a machine making money—planning for today, to get even, I guess."

"But all that time. All those years."

"I kept putting it off, telling myself I didn't know which one to kill. Which one came back that night? Which one used the knife on me? I didn't know."

"And you hated me . . . for crying out."

"Not hate. I've thought of little else except you, knowing you were the last . . . knowing you were the only one I'd love if I lived a thousand years."

He put his hand to her neck, running his fingers into her hair.

"Is it true?" he asked. "What Steve said about Louise?"

"Yes. Steve married me to give the child a name. That was all the love he could give me." She paused, weighing the words before she said them. "The only love I've had, I've given to myself, pretending it was you."

"Out here by our tree?"

"Yes."

"I'm sorry."

"But what now?" she asked. "Do you leave again?"

"I'm not a man, not really. Why should I stay?"

"We have a child. I haven't done too well alone. Perhaps together. . . ."

"Yes," he agreed. "Perhaps. . . ."

MORE BEST-SELLING MYSTERY AND SUSPENSE FROM PINNACLE

☐ **40-619-3 PAYMENT DEFERRED by C. S. Forester** $1.95
A mild-mannered man is driven to the ultimate act of despair by hopeless debt—but his secret haunts his every thought and deed. A superb psychological thriller by one of the world's most eminent storytellers.

☐ **40-529-4 THE ZODIAC KILLER by Jerry Weissman** $2.25
A novel of terrifying suspense based on the still-unsolved San Francisco murders of 1968–69.

☐ **40-665-7 MURDER IN THE KITCHEN by Fred Halliday** $2.50
Meet Stanley Delphond, the outrageous gourmet detective known for his epicurean tastes in wine, food, and bizarre crime. "Suspenseful, erotic, witty!"—*Women's Wear Daily*

☐ **40-616-9 SHERLOCK HOLMES AND THE GOLDEN BIRD by Frank Thomas** $2.25
Join the hunt as Holmes and Watson pursue an ancient Egyptian artifact—as elusive as it is priceless—from decadent Soho to exotic Constantinople.

☐ **40-862-5 KISS...BUT NEVER TELL by Catherine Linden** $1.95
A beautiful woman becomes the helpless prey of a bizarre killer who seems to know her every thought.

☐ **40-856-0 DEVLIN'S TRIANGLE by Basil Heatter** $1.75
A fabulous yacht disappears in the Bermuda Triangle, and investigator Tim Devlin gets caught between the devil and the deep blue sea.

☐ **40-396-8 THE GOLD MACHINE by Martin Davies** $1.95
A sexy, Sting-like $6 million computer caper—stolen gold, blackmail, and abduction.

Buy them at your local bookstore or use this handy coupon:
Clip and mail this page with your order

PINNACLE BOOKS, INC.—Reader Service Dept.
2029 Century Park East, Los Angeles, CA 90067

Please send me the book(s) I have checked above. I am enclosing $_____ (please add 75¢ to cover postage and handling). Send check or money order only—no cash or C.O.D.'s.

Mr./Mrs./Miss _____
Address _____
City _____ State/Zip _____

Please allow four weeks for delivery. Prices subject to change without notice.